Loyalty Is Blind

Loyalty Is Blind

Loyalty Is Blind

Nautical Publishing

Copyright 2015 by Kenneth Chisholm Loyalty is Blind

All rights reserved. No part of this book may be reproduced in any form or by electronic or mechanical means, including information storage and retrieval systems without permission in writing from the publisher, except by a reviewer who may quote brief passages in review.
First Edition April 2015
Printed in the United States of America
This is a work of fiction. Names, characters, places, and incidents either are products of the author's imagination or are used fictitiously. Any similarity to any events or locales or persons, living or dead, is entirely coincidental.

Nautical Publishing

Contact us if you would like to get published or if you have ideas. We also have ghostwriters for hire along with other services.
Contact us nauticalpublishing@yahoo.com
Like us on Facebook
www.facebook.com/nauticalpublishing

Loyalty Is Blind

Loyalty Is Blind

Chapter 1

June 15, 2016

It was a warm night during the summer in Boston. A group of hustlers were outside of the Academy Homes Projects, rolling dice and drinking. Stacks of money lay on the rugged concrete ground surrounded by a circle of fresh Adidas sneakers, liquor bottles, and blunt ashes, on the side of a project building. Bugs flew around the cracked street light in the parking lot full of luxurious cars with their doors wide open. A plethora of gritty rap music could be heard blasting out of each car that had chicken heads and hustlers sitting on, in, or around each car. People were sitting on their front stoops with their doors wide open watching the dice game that was lit up by the headlights of Power's Benz. The smell of good weed was in the air as sounds of laughter, jokes, music and car engines revving filled the air.

"Four, fifty six, here I come!" Bills yelled as he shook three dice in his hand, holding a half drank bottle of Henny in his other hand.

Bills tossed the dice over the stacks and it rolled onto the concrete and and bounced off of the building, each dice jumbled around until they landed flat on the ground revealing three numbers. 4-5-6.

"Yea! Pay up! Let me get that!" Bills yelled as he dapped his two best friends, Reign and Power, with his pinky, ring, and middle finger, holding is index and thumb together.

That's how Boston dudes dapped each other, with the threes, for the three stripes on Adidas. They never gave the trigger finger to anyone they loved.

Bills scooped up the stack of money and pulled it under him, claiming his prize.

Everyone knew Bills was cool and liked to crack jokes, but he had an anger problem when someone tried to take advantage of him. Bills was only 5'6 at 26 years old, so he always felt people were underestimating him because of his size even though people rarely did.

"C'mon man run that back." Reign said. "Shut your bootleg Ginuwine lookin' ass up and put some bread up.

Reign threw some stacks onto the ground by the feet of his best friend Bills.

"Shut your bald ass up." Bills said in a joking tone as he shook the dice. "All that muscle you got don't make you no better at this game here boy."

"Let me get in there." Power butted in. "This nigga Bills always talking shit. I bet Reign got you on this one."

Power dropped his easy earned stacks in the middle of the dice game.

"If that's really what you want." Bills said, still shaking the dice. "Just 'cause we The Cipher don't mean I won't take y'all money." Bills joked.

"Let's go man." Power said, waving Bills off.

That's when Sylph walked by. Sylphia Lauren, was beautiful with creamy light brown honey skin. She had juicy full lips with a slight slant in her eyes, which made her look kind of Asian. Her hair was long and brown. She had a natural body that would put these video girl's to shame. She had on some big expensive Gucci shades.

Sylph looked at Power next to Reign. *Damn he's so Perfect,* Sylph thought to herself.

Loyalty Is Blind

Sylph looked Power up and down from his Basketball Equipments Adidas, all the way up to his fresh designed braids. She loved his caramel skin and his hazel eyes.

After the dice game Power, Sylph, Reign, and Bills went to Power's house. Power called a team meeting, he had some things he needed to talk about with them. Sylph cooked dinner for them, and they all sat around the mahogany table eating their food.

***

"So, what's up Power?" Sylph asked, not knowing if she was really ready for this meeting.

"We all gotta talk. Shits still good, but one thing gotta change," Power said.

"Aight nigga, so what is it?" Bills asked.

"I was thinking and we gotta keep Love out of everythin', she be in too much shit."

Bills sighed, Reign sucked his teeth, Sylph shot Power a glare. They were all getting tired of Power's insecurities when it came to Sylph's safety.

"Are you fucking serious Power?" Sylph spat.

"I don't want you in all this shit." Power stated sharply.

"Fuck you Power. You really need to grow the fuck up and realize that I am a grown ass woman. I'm gonna do whatever the fuck I want."

"Not wit' me you aint. My mom died over this shit, because somebody was trying to get at my pops. I couldn't forgive myself if I ever let that happen to you."

"I gave you everything Power, I gave you me! And you just kicked me to the curb like some side hoe."

Loyalty Is Blind

"Listen, I'm sorry but-"

"First you fuck me, then you tell me you don't want me, now you tellin' me I can't be part of the team. What the fuck."

"It aint like that Love!"

"Do not call me that name. You don't love me."

Those words stung Power. Reign and Bills were really getting sick of Sylph and Power's dramatic soap opera shit. Reign actually liked and appreciated that Sylph always wanted to help them. He felt that she was a grown ass woman and should be able to make her own choices. Bills really didn't care what Sylph's fast ass did, if she wanted to run with the big boys, cool. But no matter what, he always rolled with his boys, right or wrong.

"Power. Love's a grown ass woman. She came up wit' us. I mean, how long you gon be on this shit, she obviously aint gon change her mind." Reign said.

"I don't give a fuck bout any of that shit. I'm saying I don't want her round this shit no more. From now on, shit changing."

Power's mind was made up.

"I feel you Power. I'm down wit' whatever you say," Bills said.

"I'm not a fuckin baby. I'm a twenty-six year old woman. I helped you a lot, I would do anything for you guys. I aint leaving for nothing."

"Chill yo ass out and-"

"Fuck you! Do you understand how I feel about you? Do you know how you make me feel with all the bullshit you say to me? Do you know what you did to me when you treated me like shit?"

Loyalty Is Blind

Power didn't know what to say, he sighed as he rubbed his face. Sylph stormed out of the room. Reign sighed and followed her. She raced out of Power's house, to her car.

"Love, wait up!" Reign called out, while jogging up to her.

Sylph ignored him and got in her car. Reign opened the passenger's door and hopped in. Sylph put her head on the steering wheel and cried.

"Why does he do this to me?"

"It's a'ight, he just loves you so much. He don't want you in no shit."

"He doesn't love me. You never do what he did to someone you love."

"I really don't know what to say. Patience leads to benefit. Sometimes people don't know what they got, they never notice the love that was there the whole time."

Sylph wiped away her tears. She thought about what Reign said.

She needed rest, all of this was stressing her out.

"I'm gonna go get some rest."

"A'ight, you be easy Love. I'll be at the crib if you need me."

Sylph let out a frustrated sigh as she wiped away more tears. She leaned over and kissed Reign on the cheek, and said.

"Thanks Reign, goodnight."

Reign nodded, threw up the peace sign and got out the car.

Loyalty Is Blind

Loyalty Is Blind

Chapter 2

Ten years prior, March 3, 2006

It was 3 a.m. in the morning in the quiet Suburbs. Well at least white people thought it was quiet. Those damn crickets had Power's head fucked up. Power tried to sleep when he heard a loud crash from the front door. He could only think of one thing, a raid.

Power did what his father always told him to do in this situation. He ran and climbed to the secret compartment in the ceiling. Power waited as he heard people run through his house, and then Power's heart dropped. He thought about his mom. All he could do was pray to himself, *Allah, please protect my mom.*

Power listened to the muffled sounds of people rummaging through the house. He couldn't hear any voices. After about 10 minutes. He heard one loud gunshot, and then silence.

It didn't hit Power, he didn't know what to feel yet, his mind still in denial. Power waited for what felt like an hour, and then he got out of the compartment. When he entered the hallway, he sensed something was fucked up. Before he stepped in his mother's room, he saw her hand hanging in the doorway. He calmly walked to the front of the door and was lost of words. All he could do was shed a tear and hold his mother's hand. He took a few deep breaths, and then went and picked up the phone. Most 16 year old kids would have dialed 911, but Power was taught at a young age that you don't talk to police. The justice system just makes things worse. Power called his father, Waters.

Loyalty Is Blind

He still couldn't digest everything that was happening. The house was dead silent. All Power could do was shiver and cry for his mom as he waited for his dad to get home.

Waters finally pulled into the driveway. He walked in and spotted his son holding his moms head in his lap. Power's mom had a large hole in her head. Pieces of her skull and brains were on the floor next to her son with tears in his eyes. Power tried to remember her without the hole in her head. Power looked up at his father, and asked one question.

"Why?"

Waters saw the tears in his son's eyes. Waters gave his son a simple real answer.

"It's life son."

Power didn't understand what his father was talking about. Power felt like Waters never gave him good advice because Waters always wanted to maintain a cool calm mood around Power. Waters never connected with Power on an emotional level. He provided everything for Power financially but not emotionally. Power didn't care how much things his father would buy him with drug money. He wanted a father and he needed one now more than ever.

From then on, nothing in life would hurt Power more. Being a sixteen year old boy, losing his mom to a game he never played, was the worst loss in his past and future. From then on bodies were just casualties of war and a waste of human life. His mom never hurt anyone in any way. She never sold drugs. That was all Power's father, Waters' business. Power couldn't understand how Waters could ever put his mother in harm's way. Power promised from that day on that he would never let any woman he had any type of feelings for be affected by the choices he made in life.

Chapter 3

Waters had just finished counting his money in his apartment in Academy Homes Projects at 3 a.m. in the morning. Cash sat neatly arranged in high piles on his glass coffee table. Waters grabbed each stack of money one by one, and placed it in a duffel bag, filling it up. He zipped the duffel bag closed and lifted it off of the floor by the straps. He placed it over his shoulder and headed to the front door. He opened his front door and locked it behind himself. He walked down the walkway of the projects and into the driveway. He took his keys out of his pocket and unlocked the door of his Benz. He opened the car door and tossed the bag in the passenger seat. He always took his cash to his safe house in the suburbs. When Waters pulled out of the parking lot he didn't notice Joke and Donny waiting in a dark car on a back street.

"There goes that nigga Waters." Joker said as he cocked his .9mm back.

Donny was fidgeting.

"So exactly what's the plan man?"

"We know Waters aint there. We just go in his house and wait for him. Then we tie his ass up and get him to tell us where he keeps his money."

Donny punched his fist and said.

"C'mon man let's do this man!"

"Calm your excited ass down and be quiet. His son will most likely be there. We gonna have to tie his ass up too. Don't make me regret bringing your crazy ass. I only need you to pick the front lock and shut the hell up. Let me do

Loyalty Is Blind

everything you just watch my back and don't do anything stupid. When we get this niggas money you can buy all the coke you can sniff."

"I know man I got you. C'mon." Donny said impatient as he picked his bag of supplies off of the car floor.

Joker and Donny got out of the car and quietly closed the doors. They crept around the shadows of the back road and hopped a fence to Academy Homes Projects. They scanned the parking lot and windows real quick, giving it a quick look up and down and left and right. They saw no sign of anyone awake. They moved as fast and quiet as they could to the front stoop of Waters' apartment. Donny pulled his lock picking equipment out of his bag and his shaky hands took only moments to pick the lock. Joker quietly entered the dark apartment first, aiming his .9mm into the darkness. Donny followed behind him, entering the apartment. Donny started to close the door behind him but it creaked. Joker looked back at him and put his finger over his lips, signaling for Donny to be quiet. Donny slowly pushed the door but didn't close it all the way so it didn't make noise. Joker has done this a few times before so he stayed calm. Donny stood behind him as he looked around the dark living room. He saw no one, so they quietly crept into Power's room. Power laid on his bed in a deep sleep.

"Wakey wakey nigga." Joker said loud enough to wake Power.

Power sat up fast, being awoken to a gun pointing in his face. Donny turned the light on in Power's room and he pushed the door halfway closed behind himself.

"Don't make any noise." Joker explained. "You'll be a'ight. We just want your father's paper. So where's it at?"

Loyalty Is Blind

Power was confused and shocked. He had no idea what was happening and he really didn't even know where his dad was or where his money was at. Power was scared.

"Uh-um, I have no idea. For real."

"He's lying!" Donny yelled, he dug his hand into his bag of supplies and pulled out a knife. "This dude knows where it's at. Tell us where it's at!"

Joker looked back at Donny, "Shut your loud ass up before someone hears us."

"I swear, I don't know." Power said. "But I know where some dope is. I got some in my top drawer."

Joker rushed over to Power's dresser and slid open the top drawer. He found a bag of dope, about 15 grams. Joker picked the dope up and tossed it on the floor next to Power.

"You think this is a game nigga? You wanna get shot? That aint no real amount!"

Joker was furious. He swung the gun at Power's head and gun butted him.

"Ah!" Power yelled in pain.

***

Bills and Reign were walking around outside of Academy Homes Projects at three in the morning, stealing shit from cars as Bills talked about cartoons.

"That nigga, Goku, is a gangsta'. Can't nobody fuck wit' him. Everybody around the universe knows what time it is wit' my nigga Goku."

"You crazy, nigga. Nobody cares about your stupid ass cartoons." Reign sighed.

Bills suddenly stopped dead in his tracks. Reign stopped with him. Bills looked straight ahead. He saw two men

Loyalty Is Blind

jumping a side fence of Academy Homes Projects. Reign looked to where Bills was looking and also saw. Reign grabbed Bills and pulled him behind two big trash barrels. They sat there in silence until the men kept it moving. They stood up from hiding.

"Who the fuck were they?" Bills asked.

"I don't know. I thought it was the police but it was just niggas." Reign shrugged.

Bills had a funny feeling. They walked out into the parking lot and saw no sign of the men. They continued to walk toward Bills' apartment. That's when they heard someone yelling.

"What the fuck is that?" Bills asked.

"Sound like some yelling nigga. It's nothing," Reign said as he shrugged it off.

"It sounds like its coming from over there, let's check." Bills said pointing to Power's apartment.

"Hell no nigga! I say we mind our own business and keep it moving," Reign said.

"What if someone needs help?"

"So!? What the hell that gotta do with us?"

"We can't just walk by and do nuttin'."

"Are you serious?" Reign yelled looking at his friend like he was crazy.

"Someone could be in trouble. Waters or Power never be loud at night."

Reign's jaw dropped. "You're serious." Reign slapped his head. "See, you watch too much cartoons and wanna fly around like Gookah and save all these niggaz and shit! You 15 years old. Act like it."

"First of all, his names Goku. And second of all, this my

hood. I gotta know everythin that's goin down round this bitch. I gotta know why niggas is screamin at 3 in the morning," Bills said.

They were silent, and then they heard Power yelling in pain.

"Well I'm gonna find out what's going on," Bills said as he pulled a .22 out of his waistband, cocked it and walked toward Power's apartment.

Reign sighed, and then followed. They walked to Power's front door and noticed it was cracked open. They could hear what was going on inside.

***

"Ah!" Power yelled in pain as some blood trickled down his forehead.

"Tie this nigga up," Joker told Donny.

Donny put his knife back in his bag of supplies and pulled some rope out. He walked over to Power and tied his hands behind his back. Power didn't resist as Donny tied his feet and pushed him off of his bed and to the ground, by the foot of his bed. Donny went back into his bag and pulled the knife back out as he glared at Power.

"I been watching your dad's schedule. I know it should be a while till he gets back. I'm fine with that I can wait all night for him." Joker teased.

Power was defenseless. He had a flurry of emotions. He didn't know what to do. Donny finished tying Power up.

Loyalty Is Blind

Loyalty Is Blind

Chapter 4

Bills and Reign slowly entered Power's apartment. They could hear Joker and Donny talking to Power. Bills and Reign crept through Power's living room using Joker and Donny's talking and yelling to hide the sounds of their movement. Bills and Reign made eye contact in the dark room only lit by the moonlight sneaking through the shades. They nodded at each other and crept over to Power's room door. They stood outside and listened quietly, making sure they didn't step into the light coming from the crack of Power's door being open. Bills could hear that Joker mentioned he had a gun. Bills had to assume it was a bigger gun than his little .22. Bills and Reign both knew that they still had the advantage. They had the element of surprise. They had to react as soon as possible to keep that advantage. Bills could see Joker and Donny's shadows on the carpet floor in front of him so he had a pretty accurate estimation of exactly where they were both standing in Power's room. Bills peeked his head into the doorway and looked at the layout of the room. He could see that Donny and Joker had their backs completely turned to them as Joker held the gun aimed at Power.

    Bills dashed into the room as he pushed the door to the side. He quickly aimed his gun up at the back of Joker's neck. Bills pulled the trigger as fast as he could.

    Bang! Bang! Bang!

    He let of three shots, the shots were deafening in Power's small room. The bullets entered into the back of Joker's neck and ricochet up his neck bone and rattled around his brain.

Loyalty Is Blind

Joker's body fell to the ground next to Power, lifeless. Power ducked, still not knowing what was happening. As Bills ran in the room Reign swung a heavy hook towards Donny's face. He connected and Donny stumbled back and tripping over Joker's dead body. Reign went to rush Donny but Donny quickly stood up swinging the knife at Reign. Reign backed up and stood next to Bills who was aiming the gun at Donny. Donny stood over Power holding his knife up.

"Back the fuck up or I'll stab him!" Donny yelled.

Power's heart was beating faster than he ever knew it could. Bills' .22 was only a 5 shot. Bills only shot three, so he had two bullets left. Bills really wasn't even aware of how many times he shot, he only knew he had at least one bullet left because the hammer wasn't lodged back. They were all in a bad situation. Joker's body laid next to Power, with the .9mm still in a weak grasp of Joker's lifeless hand. Power looked down at his tied up feet next to the gun, then up to the knife shining in the light of his room in Donny's hand. Donny was breathing heavy as sweat rushed out of his pores on his face. Bills didn't want to miss a shot and have Donny rush them with his knife or even go for the gun in Joker's hand, which was closer to him. Donny raised the knife like he was going to stab Power, and Bills reacted. He pulled the trigger.

The loud sound of the gunshot blasted off of the walls of the small room. The .22 bullet hit Donny in the chest. Donny stumbled back. Reign dashed forward, leaped over Power, and tackled Donny to the ground. Reign managed to get on top of Donny and grab his wrist with both hands, making sure he couldn't stab him. Bills dropped his empty gun on Power's carpet and ran to aid Reign. Bills kicked Donny in his head repeatedly. Donny grunted in pain as the tip of Bills'

Loyalty Is Blind

shell toe crashed into his face and head over and over, spewing blood from Donny's face with each kick. Donny was getting weaker from being shot and from each kick Bills was delivering. Donny's grip on the knife was getting weaker. It slipped out of his. Reign grabbed the knife, lifted it high in the air and plunged it deep into Donny's neck. Blood shot out of Donny's neck and mouth as he gargled blood and gasped for air.

Reign held the knife in Donny's neck as his body twitched and contorted in pain until Donny's body slowed down and died. Bills and Reign sat there in silence. Reign still sat on Donny's body holding the knife into his neck as he was breathing heavy. Power looked at the two people that just saved his life. Bills wiped the sweat off of his forehead, walked over to Power, and untied him. Reign stood up, while leaving the knife in Donny's neck.

"I really don't know what to say, but thanks." Power said.

Bills picked his gun up and put it in his pocket. Then walked over to Joker, took the .9mm out of his hand, and put it in his waist band. He also took Joker's small dookie rope chain off and put it over his own neck.

Reign looked at Power. "You better not tell no one. I don't even know you and your ass might snitch on us. Tell me why we shouldn't kill your ass too?"

"Man shut up, Reign." Bills said. "He's just going crazy cuz he watched me kill that nigga."

"You killed him? That was me." Reign spat.

"Nigga I killed him wit' my accurate aim and quick reflexes. I'm like *Vash the Stampede* wit' the guns nigga."

"Who the fuck is that?" Reign yelled

Reign and Bills argued with each other. Power looked

Loyalty Is Blind

back and forth at the two people, feeling kind of confused as to why they would be arguing at a time like this.

"Yo!" Power yelled, interrupting their fight. "We gotta figure some shit out. We sitting in a room with two dead bodies in it. What the fuck are we gonna do?"

Bills scratched his head like he was confused. "I don't know man. Can't your father handle this shit?"

With everything going on, Power didn't even think of calling his father.

"Good idea." Power said, grabbing his cell phone off of his dresser.

He sent his dad a text message that read: *Come here it's important.*

***

Waters was at his safe house in the suburbs when he got a text from Power. He looked at it and knew something was wrong. Waters remained calm, like he always does, and walked outside to his car. He hopped in and drove an hour to Academy Homes Projects. When he got there he walked inside and saw Reign standing at the corner with his arms crossed, Power sitting on a sofa looking at the ground, and Bills sitting on his couch with his shoes on, feet up on the arm.

"Sup big homie?" Bills said, nodding his head at Waters.

"Get your damn feet off my couch is what's up." Waters said sternly.

"Geesh." Bills said as he moved his feet to the floor and leaned forward in the chair. "That's the thanks I get for saving your son's life?"

Waters looked at Power. "Power what the fuck is going

on?"

Power looked up at his father with a dead serious look on his face, and then he stood up. Power remained silent as he turned around and walked toward his room. Waters followed him. Power pushed open his door, revealing two dead bodies. The carpet of Power's room was totally soaked in blood. Power explained what happened. Waters looked around. He felt sorry that his son had to go through such a traumatizing event for something Waters was into himself, but he would never say it out loud. He was also thankful to Reign and Bills. He walked out to the living room and looked at Reign and Bills, who was once again lying on the couch with his feet up. Waters reach into his pocket and pulled out a fat stack of money that was folded and held together by a thick rubber band.

He tossed it to Reign. "Thanks. You two split that."

Reign caught the stack and held it in his hand. He looked at the money, more than he's ever seen in his life. Bills stood up rubbing his hands together and said.

"You're welcome big homie." Bills said, with excitement.

Reign stood there looking at the money, and then he looked from the money to Waters.

"Nah," he tossed the stack back to Waters. "We don't want that, give us some dope."

"What?" Bills shouted. "Nigga you crazy! Big homie, give me the money. I'll keep all of it."

Bills hoped Waters didn't change his mind about the money.

"That's a lot of money, but it will only do us good for a little while. We don't need to be good for a little while. We need stability forever."

Loyalty Is Blind

Waters actually liked what he was hearing.

"Reign, shut the fuck up. You crazy nigga. Let's take the money and get outta here." Bills said, mad.

Reign looked at his best friend. "For what. So you can blow all that away like a trickin' ass nigga? You wanna be trickin' or do you wanna be pimpin'? I'm tired of seeing these tricking ass niggas spending everything on being fresh and bitches. I'm not about that. I wanna make some real money and build some real shit with it."

Water looked Reign dead in his eyes. Reign was serious and ready. Waters was silent for a moment.

"We'll talk tomorrow." He put the money back in his pocket. "All of you clean yourselves up. Power get them a change of clothes. I'll call someone to dispose of the bodies. It's almost morning. We'll leave at daybreak and talk about everything."

Chapter 5

Waters called his connect, Wasala. He talked to him in code.

"I need your nephew to come change my carpet and paint my walls. Power's room is a mess."

"I'll send him right away. He'll negotiate the price with you."

Waters hung up.

Not too long after, Hasad walked into the house, followed by 4 other Arabic men who were holding tools, cleaning supplies, heavy duty contract trash bags and tarps. Hasad was Wasala's nephew, who he raised. Hasad grew up doing everything that was too dirty for Wasala to do. Hasad forgot how many people he killed and he was still young at the age of 21. Hasad walked into the living room and looked at Bills and Reign because they were unfamiliar faces to him. He sized them both up in his mind. Reign and Hasad locked eyes sizing each other up. They stared for a moment until Waters interrupted them.

"The bodies are in the back room,"

"Me and my men will clean it up. Wasala will negotiate the pay for this job the next time you pick up from him. Just leave for the day, when you come back the house will be back to normal."

"Sure thing." Waters nodded, then turned to his son and said, "Let's head out now."

Reign, Bills, and Power followed Waters out of the house and to the parking lot. Waters pulled his key to his Benz out and clicked the unlock button from across the parking lot, unlocking the doors to his car, parked next to Hasad's generic

Loyalty Is Blind

looking cleaning van with a business name posted on the side and the phone number. They got into his car. Bills looked around the car amazed. He's never been in a car so expensive. He was shocked to even be able to adjust the heat in the back and move the seats back and forth.

Waters pulled into the parking lot of a nice restaurant. They all stepped out of the car one by one, and walked inside. They were seated, and ordered their food. They ate for a while and made small talk until Waters broke the ice.

"So you wanna start hustling out here?" Waters asked.

"No. I don't wanna start. I been hustling all my life. I just wanna take it to the next level." Reign answered.

"This nigga aint no damn hustler." Bills joked, with food still in his mouth. "He just runs around telling everyone he knows me so they respect him."

Waters ignored Bills. "Well I most definitely owe you a favor. You guys saved my son's life. I'll front you something. If you bring me my money back, we'll do business. If not, you keep the money and that will be my favor to you."

"I appreciate your favor and I respect your hustle. But I think we can make you even bigger out here." Reign said.

Waters dropped his fork on his plate and showed a hint of a smirk, then said. "I thank you for helping my son. I highly doubt that there's anything you young bloods could do to benefit me."

"Let me ask you a question."

"Shoot."

"How many people owe you money that don't pay you?"

"A good amount," Waters shrugged, "but that's the game. Everyone has people that owes them. You just cut those dudes out. It's almost like paying to not fuck with bum ass dudes that aren't consistent or loyal customers."

"You're an OG, a big homie. People respect your hustle, but they know that you won't do anything to them if you don't pay them because you are *above all of that*. Well I ain't above wilding out and shooting a couple of niggas. You can only hustle so long without hurting someone until no one respects you and just comes and straight up robs you. Why do you think them dudes that we bodied came at you?"

Waters had to admit Reign was right. Waters made money but he never got into violence and that had to change if he wanted to protect his business.

"I like what I'm hearing." Waters nodded. "I'll throw you something tonight."

"I'm in this too." Power butted in.

"No the hell you're not Power. I'm not having you in any of this." Waters said sternly.

"Well I'm sorry dad but you already put me in this. It's your fault that I almost got killed and that mom already is dead." Power said trying to hide his anger. "Now I'm telling you I'm in this. I'm not just being Waters son who does nothing. I'm not gonna mark myself as some target. I'm riding out and grinding out." Power explained.

"Don't worry," Bills swallowed food. "I'll look out for your son. Your son is safe wit' me. I'm like a ninja. Can't nobody fuck wit me."

Everyone was silent for a moment.

"Well we need a name between the thre of us. Oh. I got a good one. How about the *Aketsuki*?"

"What the hell are you talking about?" Reign asked because he was not feeling like hearing Bills' shit.

"Me, you, and Power. We need a team name if we all

Loyalty Is Blind

gonna be grinding out together. How about Team Seven?" Bills came up with a bunch of crazy names, but everyone ignored them. Waters paid for the food and left the restaurant. He took them out shopping to get some new shoes and clothes. When Waters got a text from Hasad saying he was finished they went back to Academy Homes Projects and walked inside the apartment. It looked like nothing ever happened there. Everyone sat around Waters living room and then Waters took a deep breath.

"I've been thinking about your proposal Reign. And I'm sorry, but I can't put you on. I know if I put you on Power will get involved, and I can't do that to my son. I already lost his mother to this game. I won't lose my son." Waters pulled out a wad of cash and tossed it to Bills. "Do what you will with the money. You're a smart kid Reign. Don't waste it on this game." Waters stood up. "You guys should head back home now. Thank you for everything. Please don't tell anyone about anything you saw or heard today."

Waters walked into his room and shut his door.

Reign stood up from the couch. He gritted his teeth in disappointment as Bills smelled the stack of money like it was flowers.

"Sorry guys," Power said.

"Don't be sorry." Bills said happy. "We'll be a'ight."

"Let's spin some laps around The A." Power said.

They walked outside in the parking lot and around the projects talking.

"Don't worry about it Reign. I'll find a way to get you something to hustle." Power said.

"That would be appreciated." Reign said. "I'm tired of nickel and diming."

Loyalty Is Blind

Bills was rubbing his hands spending the money in his head. A group of little kids and teenagers ranged from 11 to 13 were standing on the fence around the projects. There were at least two dozen of them. They always were riding around the projects on their bikes. They spent a majority of their time sitting at the entrances asking unfamiliar faces where they were from. They would be on the sidewalks and the streets around Academy Homes trying to act tough and start problems. They usually didn't start up too much problems with the people that lived in Academy Homes. The kids surrounded Bills excited to see him. All of the kids looked up to Bills. He treated them all like his little brothers and would always take his time to chill with them. Bills broke off from Reign and Power to talk with the kids. Power and Reign spoke alone.

"It shouldn't be too hard to get our own dope." Power said.

"Why don't we just pay someone else to grab dope off of your father?" Reign asked.

"He doesn't mess with too many people. He trusts no one."

"So we just pay someone that's already buying from him."

"Sounds like a good idea," Power nodded his head. "We would be paying a little more than my father would give it to us for but it could work."

They watched Bills wrestling with the kids and playing around with them.

"Any idea who could do that for us?" Reign asked.

"I'll think about it. I should be able to find someone who wouldn't tip off my dad to what we're doing."

Loyalty Is Blind

They watched Bills dap up some of the kids and walk back over to them. They continued to walk around the projects.

"Well, we might as well get our plays up." Power said. "I got a little of my dad's dope that i found on the floor. It's only a little bit though. I was gonna give it back to my pops but I just never got around to it. So we should just flip it to get some clientele."

"Sounds like a plan. I know all the dope heads around here." Reign said.

"This is where it all starts." Bills said. "From now on we can't let noone break our cipher. Matter of fact, that's our name, *The Cipher*."

"Whatever Bills." Reign waved him off. "We can be The Cipher if you shut up."

Chapter 6

"It should be easy. Fiends be walking all over this bitch," Reign said.

The Cipher all looked at each other. Bills shrugged with a look like, *Let's go.*

It was getting dark outside. The streetlights had just turned on minutes ago. They saw fiends walking around. They spotted an OG fiend named MudBone. MudBone swore he knew everything about anything. Reign knew MudBone because he smoked crack with his parents back in the day. Reign and Bills used to stay away from him because he would talk so much and Bills would argue with him about the most random shit. Bills didn't know how to shut up and neither did MudBone. But today, they had to talk business with him.

"A'yo, MudBone," Reign said.

"What's happ'nin', young bloods?"

Power and Bills stood silently behind Reign, who wasted no time to hit MudBone with the question.

"Who needs some dope around here?"

"I don't do no dope."

Reign gave MudBone a crooked look. For some odd reason some fiends didn't like to admit that they were fiends, especially to younger people. They were in denial or just didn't want to look like less of a person, but he didn't trick Reign for one second.

"Aint nobody asked if you do dope. I thought you knew everythin' goin' on around here. So I just asked who needs some."

Loyalty Is Blind

Both of Reign's parents were fiends. He knew how to deal with them. Reign knew MudBone would want all the dope they had as long as he could portray his false identity to them.

"Oh yea, I know people that do it. How much you got anyways?"

Reign pulled out the bag of dope, which now was bagged up in half grams individually. MudBone's heart jumped. It did every time he saw dope. MudBone thought about doing the dope. He couldn't wait for his next fix. He would kill just to feel good for a brief moment.

"How much you want a gram?" MudBone asked, trying his best to sound calm.

"Less than other niggas that's sellin'. We The Cipher. We got it for the low." Bills said.

"Well Juan, Chino, and them *730 King* niggas got it for pretty low right now."

Other competition was the only thing Power was worried about. Power didn't want to get in anybody else way or ruffle any feathers. He didn't want people to look at him like he was competition, or trying to step on their feet. Juan has been doing his thing for a little while now, he had everything on lock in Academy Homes when it came strictly to hitting the fiends. If the Cipher just popped up and started making moves the 730s might take it offensive. All the teens in the whole projects respected 730s. All of the young bucks wanted to be down with them, and Juan was even getting his dope from one of Power's father's under bosses. Power thought about everything, and came up with a few hazardous conclusions.

"Yo, forget about that shit. We aint sellin' nothin." Power

yelled.

Reign and Bills looked at Power. MudBone's heart skipped a beat because he wanted that dope. He couldn't wait for it to get in his system. How could they just show the dope, say they had it for cheap, then just cut him off like that?

"You sure Power? I know people that want some." MudBone said.

"Nah OG. We aint got none." Power lied.

MudBone shot Power a crooked glare, and then walked away.

"What the fuck wrong wit' you?" Bills yelled, furious.

Bills really needed the money that Power just made walk away. Bills needed every dime and Power just didn't understand that. Power's father was rich and could buy him anything. Bills didn't have that luxury. He was dirt poor. Bills lived with his mother and his little brother Maleek. Bills slept on a small mattress with no sheet on the floor with his little brother Maleek.

"I was just thinkin'. My dad fuck's wit Juan's peoples. Let's not start no shit with them."

"Man, fuck all that bullshit. Them niggas don't own The A. They won't be mad over one fiend." Reign said.

"Whatever. Let's go get this dope off," Power suggested.

They walked around Academy Homes. They pretty much knew all the fiends around that area. They handed out a few packs and got a couple dollars.

***

Juan, Chino, Nico and a couple other 730s sat on their stoop, drinking Henny as Terror Squads *Watch Out*, played on the stereo.

You look, I look, you invite it, I took. I forever wearin' it you know stone cold crook what's truth, what's lie? Who's peoples, who's spy? It's life or death, chose live or die. Ultimatums who made 'em, why do we even exist? When we die is there heaven or is it total blackness? For any touch there's a feelin', touch and y'all felt. We can exchange shots until our chambers melt. There's mad tension in the air(mad tension in the air) over one man's stare, you wanna dare.

The 730s were mostly Spanish, with a few brothers down with them. Power's father, Waters, knew of 730s. He liked them because they brought in a good amount of money and kept people away from Academy Homes Projects. As of that moment Juan was running 730s. Juan used to bully other smaller crews or people he knew couldn't stand up to him. He sold some dope so had a descent amount of money to his name.

MudBone walked up to them, and said, "Yo Juan."

"Sup, OG?"

"Them lil' niggas in The Cipher talkin' 'bout, they got that shit lower then y'all 730s got it for."

"Who? And they said what??" Jaun asked feeling a little disrespected.

"Them youngins Power, Bills, and Reign, they said they The Ciper now. They said fuck y'all 730 niggas. They pulled out a bag of dope right in front of me, talkin' bout they takin' shit over now."

Juan stood up. "Where these niggas at?"

Chino stood up next to Juan then said. "Chill out Juan. That's Water's son and them."

"Fuck that. You think I give a damn?" Juan asked.

Loyalty Is Blind

"I'm just lettin' you know 'cuz we cool Juan. You think I can get a 20 bag for lookin' out?" MudBone begged.

"Give this nigga a 20 bag," Juan said, pointing to Nico. Nico gave MudBone a free 20 of dope. Nico would do anything to impress Juan. He looked up to him because Juan flashed his money around. Being young and naive Nico thought that was cool. Nico was 18 Juan was 27 so Nico would do whatever to impress him.

"Got you Juan." Nico said handing MudBone a 20 bag.

MudBone quickly snatched the dope and walked away. Chino looked at MudBone's back as he bounced away with his fiend bop, happy he got free dope.

"Fuck that old ass nigga. He don't know what he talkin' 'bout. He just wanted some free dope," Chino said.

Chino knew Juan always blew up on shit for no reason. And Chino liked those Cipher kids. He respected how Power carried himself, and didn't want any trouble with Waters. Chino couldn't stand how Juan handled things, especially how he treated Nico. Nico was Juan's 18 year old crash dummy. Juan knew that Nico looked up to him, and would do anything to impress him, so Juan used that to his advantage. 730s had strength in numbers, but were unorganized with Juan leading them.

"MudBone aint never came to me wit' no bullshit before," Juan said.

"Man, fuck them Cipher niggas. Let's go find them niggas right now!" Nico yelled.

Chino sighed. He was starting to get sick of Juan bullying weaker people.

"C'mon y'all they round here somewhere," Juan said.

Loyalty Is Blind

Chapter 7

The Cipher was walking when they saw the 730s walking towards them. They noticed Juan, Nico, and Chino with six other people. Power and the crew weren't hard to find in the projects. MudBone already gave them their location. Power remembered Chino from back in the day when Chino used to steal cars, and break in houses. Chino was eighteen. He's always seemed like a cool, humble kid. He even would dap The Cipher when he would see them and buy weed off of them sometimes.

"What these niggas doin'?" Reign asked.

"I don't know, but they walkin' right to us. They probably want some weed." Bills said

The Cipher and the 730s stopped right in front of each other.

"Sup?" Reign asked, with a nod towards Juan.

Juan said nothing. He mean mugged The Cipher. "Y'all niggas out here talkin shit?"

The Cipher all jerked their heads back and looked like *What the fuck?* They knew that they never said a word about the 730s, but The Cipher wasn't about to cop no pleas.

"Niggas aint never said a damn thing about y'all niggas. If we did, we would have said it right to you," Power said in a cool tone.

"Well MudBone's talkin' about y'all niggas runnin' 'round here sayin' that you takin' this over, and you got shit for lower than us."

Bills laughed. "Listen man, shit wasn't like that. This nigga MudBone just-"

Loyalty Is Blind

"Nigga, shut up! Run your pockets!" Juan yelled interrupting Bills.

Chino sighed, and then wiped his face with his hand.

"Who the fuck you talkin to nigga?" Reign yelled.

"Y'all lil' niggas is really brave, but that's the type of shit that gets you killed nigga," Juan said, pointing at Reign.

"Aight tough guys, aint gon' be no more talkin'. If y'all niggas wanna go, let's go. Aint nobody wanna sit here and waste words," Power said ready for whatever.

Juan was mad that these little niggas wouldn't just back down. Every other time, Juan could just scare younger people on sight. Not these Cipher kids though.

"Nico, fuck one of these niggas up!" Juan yelled, pointing at the Cipher.

Nico stepped in front of Juan. Reign laughed as he looked directly in Nico's eyes. He didn't care if Nico had 2 years and a couple inches on him. Reign knew he would tear Nico up.

"Any one of us will shoot the ones wit' this bitch ass nigga," Power said.

Nico looked at Reign and could just see that choosing Reign to fight was a very bad idea. Reign just looked like he was ready to take someone's head off. So Nico looked at Power and Bills. Power did just call him a bitch ass nigga, basically challenging him. Power looked tough too. Bills was small and skinny. He just looked like he couldn't hang with Nico. Nico had much more height and weight.

"C'mon nigga," Nico said, pointing at Bills.

The Cipher all laughed at Nico's choice. That right there said something about all of the 730s. Juan started to feel like he was weak because of Nico's choice. Chino raised an eye,

Loyalty Is Blind

mad at Nico.

"Man, let's do this shit," Bills said, as he took off the gold rope and handed it to Power.

How's this lil nigga got jewelry like that already? Chino thought as he looked at the rope. Chino smirked, admiring the little niggas.

"Fuck this punk ass nigga up Bills," Power said as Bills walked up to Nico.

Nico put his fists up. Bills smirked, and quickly put up his guard, like he was Bruce Leeroy or something.

The 730s looked at Bills like he was a clown.

"Get 'em Nico!" Juan yelled.

Nico took little steps toward Bills, and Bills bounced around Nico swaying left and right every few moments.

This lil' nigga movin' like he know Kung Fu. Chino thought to himself with a grin.

Nico swung at Bills. Bills dodged Nico easy. He dashed around him and hit him with a quick blow to his ribs. Nico almost coughed.

He's fast! Nico thought as he began to regret choosing to fight Bills.

Power and Reign looked at each other sharing a smile. They already knew the outcome of this fight. Bills was too quick. Power, Bills, and Reign always fought with each other, just to stay on point. Bills speed was nothing nice.

Nico stumbled back, and swung at Bills again. Bills dodged, backed up, and bounced around Nico, with a half-smile on his face.

Juan was breathing heavy with anger. Chino slowly nodded his head, impressed. Nico shuffled toward Bills, who bounced around and quickly hit Nico with three strikes to his

Loyalty Is Blind

head.

Bang! Bang! Bang!

Nico stumbled back again. Bills rushed in and hit Nico in the stomach. Nico swung and connected with Bills' jaw. Bills stumbled back, but quickly got back into his bounce. They exchanged blows. Bills was to quick and dodged a lot of Nico's punches. He hit Nico up and even threw a few kicks that hit him in the chest and legs. Bills had more stamina than Nico. It was obvious to see that Bills had the upper hand in the fight. Nico was getting tired and breathing heavy. He had to grab Bills because he couldn't keep standing up with him. Nico stepped in toward Bills and Bills swung a slow haymaker.

This is my chance, Nico thought, excited.

He caught Bills' arm with both hands. Bills was too small to wrestle away from him. Nico would easily scoop him and slam him hard on the ground.

Juan's heart raced in excitement."

"Slam that lil' nigga Nico!"

He pulled Bills in toward himself to get a betted grip.

"It's over," Reign said calmly.

Nico looked into Bills' eyes. He was so happy that he finally caught Bills. Then Bills half-smiled and winked. Bills jumped into Nico, lifted his knee up and powerfully drove it deep into Nico's stomach.

Power snickered.

Nico bent over in pain. He couldn't breathe. That's when Bills' elbow came down on the back of Nico's head. His skull shook at the force of the elbow. He fell face first into the concrete. Juan and the 730s ran towards Bills. Power pulled out the .9mm, Reign pulled out the .22.

Loyalty Is Blind

The 730s stopped in their tracks.
Chino looked at the 9mm that Power was holding.
Well that's a cool 9. Where you get that from youngin'?
Chino thought to himself calmly.
Juan pulled out his .38 and pointed it at Power. None of the other 730s had a gun besides Juan and Chino.
"Y'all niggas are all bitches!" Power yelled.
Chino felt Power. Juan definitely handled ever situation wrong. Nico did make them look like bitches by picking the smallest nigga to fight, and then losing on top of that.
Chino held his .9mm at his side.
"Fuck y'all lil' niggas!" Juan yelled, embarrassed.
Suddenly, Juan felt an agonizing pain in the back of his head. Chino just pistol whipped him. The gun made a loud clunk noise as it hit the back of his head. Juan fell to the ground, unconscious next to Nico. Bills kept his guard up, Reign and Power pointed their guns at Chino. The Cipher didn't know what to do. Chino gave them a funny laugh as he held the gun to his side. He smiled so wide that they could see all of his teeth and eyes squinted.
"Y'all niggas all get outta here. Go back to the stoop, and I'll be over there in a lil' while," Chino said, waving his free hand up casually.
The 730s listened to Chino's command, and walked off.
Bills lowered his guard, and Power and Reign lowered their guns to their sides. Chino put his gun back in his waistband.
"I respect y'all lil' niggas." Chino stated.
Power and Reign put their guns away.
"No doubt, nigga." Power said, still puzzled.
Chino gave them a comforting laugh. "I can't roll wit' a

Loyalty Is Blind

nigga like Juan. He been fake since day one. Y'all niggas held up yourselves like real niggas today. I see that. We could all make real moves together."

"Word? All you did was see us fight. How could you tell if we really real niggas?" Powers asked.

"I saw a lot more than just a fight here."

"What else you see?" Bills asked, looking around.

"I see y'all took out Joker."

Oh shit! Reign thought, but his face remained cool.

"What makes you think that?" Bills asked, trying to cover up.

"Well I noticed that Joker's been missing. He used to cop his dope off me and I don't know where he's been. Then I seen y'all had his chain and his gun, and put together the fact that y'all aint never had no dope before, until Joker came up missing."

It was silent for a little.

"We didn't mean to fuck up your money," Power said apologetically.

"Fuck that little bit of bread. Y'all niggas is worth way more than that money."

"How?" Reign asked.

"Look, it's hard to find real niggas now. Y'all niggas is mos' def' real ass niggas. That nigga Joker must have done something to piss y'all off. And now y'all showed these fake niggas up," Chino said, and then pointed to Juan and Nico lying on the ground.

The Cipher agreed with Chino.

"I got a plan that could make us all a lot of money, and by the end of this shit. Y'all will be making more than me. Y'all niggas will run the whole city," Chino said, excited.

Loyalty Is Blind

The Cipher exchanged glares and thoughts.

"So wassup? Y'all down? The Cipher and The 730s could run shit," Chino said as he put his three fingers out.

730s was a loose crew. They basically just went with whoever was running shit in their crew at the time. It looks like Chino just took Juan's spot.

The Cipher all dapped Chino with the threes.

Loyalty Is Blind

Chapter 8

About a year has passed and Chino definitely stood by his word. He hooked it up for The Cipher. Chino started to get his dope off of one of Waters' under bosses, and gave each of them their own clientele. He set up Bills with all Joker's old business and then split all of Juan's old business between Reign and Power. The Cipher and Chino were making more money then they ever have.

Bills' mom was struggling a lot less, and he even started to notice how fake all of the girls were. Now that he has money, the girls just couldn't get enough of him. He didn't get any type of attention like that when he was broke. Chino and his main man Smoke would throw parties every weekend, even though The Cipher was young, they would always be invited and would show up.

Smoke was straight from the dirty south. He was tall and heavy. He had a mouth full of gold teeth with dark brown skin. He didn't like to move too much unless he had to, but he always had something to say. He had a thick southern accent, and you could always catch him saying *ya know dat*.

All of the kids their age wanted to be them. They started to become more like businessmen. Bills had control over all of the younger kids that looked up to him. He would hook them up with a little money if they needed it and take them shopping. He could send them on just about any type of mission and they would move, no question, for him. About a little over a year passed and The Cipher was being recognized as the realest little niggas in the city. That's when Waters heard about his son.

Loyalty Is Blind

    Power basically stayed in the apartment in Academy Homes by himself, though Waters aid for it. He was 18 now so Waters gave him more freedom.
    Waters was sitting in his living room in Academy Homes. He was sitting at his coffee table across from Bigz. The glass coffee table was covered with hundreds, fifties and twenty dollar bills next to Waters' ashtray which held a still smoking Cuban cigar. Waters counted out the stacks of money to make sure Bigz' money was on point. Bigz rolled with a crew called *EastSide*. Bigz would buy dope off of Waters ever now and then.
    "Damn dude, my money always been right." Bigz said, frustrated. "You always counting my money like I'm gonna short you or some shit."
    "I count everybody's money." Waters said, grabbing his cigar with his free hand and taking a drag. He blew the smoke out and said, "It aint nothin' against you brotha' I always do this so chill your ass out."
    "Whatever man, just hurry up I got plays to hit." Bigz said
    Waters waved him off and continued counting. Waters finished counting the money, leaned over in the couch he was sitting, grabbed a shoebox that had dope in it and placed it on the coffee table in front of Bigz.
    "So should I sit here and weigh this shit out finger by finger since you like to count every damn piece of cash I bring you?" Bigz asked, with an attitude.
    Waters shrugged with his cigar still clenched in his lips. "If you want,"
    Bigz shook his head, grabbed the shoe box and walked out the front door. Waters got up off the couch and walked

into Powers room. It smelled like Muslim oils but was a pretty plain room. It only had a bed and a dresser in it. He had a couple books sitting on his dresser, including the Quran, a Malcolm X biography, some street lit books. They were sitting next to a small scale he used to weigh his weed he would sell.

Waters looked around his room and then looked at Power and sternly. "Hey, son."

"'Sup pops?"

"Let me cut right to the chase. I know you and your boys out there sellin' dope and weed."

"Yea pops. I ain't even gonna lie to you."

Waters rubbed his temples. "Boy, what the fuck is your problem? You act like you need any damn money! I buy you everything you need! Now you out here risking your life!"

"Dad. It ain't about the money."

Waters twisted his face up. Was Power crazy? He hated when people say stupid, heroic, cliché shit.

"Don't give me that dumb shit! It's either that or you trying to be cool!"

"Not that either. It's something' you wouldn't understand."

"Y'all youngins' think y'all know everything at 18. Tell me what the fuck you've done and been through that I haven't!"

"My niggas…"

Waters looked at his son, who just might be crazy. "My niggas?"

Waters was silent.

"I'm riding wit' my niggas. I don't care about money or being cool."

Loyalty Is Blind

Waters didn't understand. Power was right about that.

"*Your niggas* are more important than making the right choices?"

"You just don't understand dad. All you care about is money. I never seen you with no partner. You don't got no real niggas. I could hear you and that dude Bigz talking from in my room. That aint your nigga, he's only a dollar to you and you only a dollar to him. You have no team that you break bread with. I barely see you. You don't stay here. You stay at that house on the better side of town. You come here just to check on me every now and then. My niggas, I see them every day. We ride every day."

Waters' heart was hurt though he would never admit it. He had to keep his cool attitude intact to maintain his pride. *Pride is a monster*. Waters' son grew up and realized that his friends were there more than his own father. Power's mother, Maryam, was Power's everything. She was his mentor, his best friend, his joking partner, his cook, his mother, and more. Even when Maryam was murdered, for something that Waters did, Waters still showed no emotion. He always stayed cool no matter what.

All Waters ever did was be hard on Power for no reason. No matter what Power did, Waters would always say he was wrong. All Power ever did was try and impress him. He wanted to hear those four little words *I'm proud of you*. The same words Maryam always said to Power even when it was only a noodle necklace that he made in kindergarten class. When Power brought his report card back from junior high school and Waters saw it was all A's, Waters just casually tossed report card on the table without a word. So Power gave up, he was done trying to impress other people. He only

Loyalty Is Blind

wanted to impress himself. He didn't care what Waters thought anymore. What would Waters do, ground him?

Waters didn't say a word for a moment. "Wasala is coming here soon. He wants to see you. Get dressed, we're going out."

Waters walked out of Power's room.

Wasala was Waters' connect. He was Arabic in his blood and Muslim in his soul. Wasala felt that as long as he wasn't selling drugs to Muslims there was no sin on himself. Wasala lived by the Qur'an. He prayed five times a day, every single day, and would only eat foods that were lawful in the Islamic way. Every time he would see Power, he would talk about Islam. Power respected Wasala deeply because of the way he carried himself. Even Waters would humble himself in Wasala's presence. Power would always take a shower and pray before he was about to see Wasala. Every now and then, Wasala would come from Saudi Arabia to see Waters and Power. Wasala didn't need to come to America, but he liked to see Power.

Power took a shower, got dressed in his suit, prayed, and then followed his father to a limo. Four men in black suits surrounded the limo. They looked like some type of super-secret service. One of the men opened the limo door for Waters and Power. They got in the limo and the four men got into a car behind the limo. The body guards didn't need to be around the limo anymore, it was bullet proof. Wasala sat in the seat in front of Power and Waters. Wasala's face was covered on a very long beard and he had a thick white turban on his head. Wasala looked Power in the eyes and smiled under his beard.

"Power, my young friend, how are you?" Wasala said in

49

Loyalty Is Blind

a warming voice.

"I've been very well Wasala. How have you been?"

Power was always extra well-mannered when Wasala was around. Wasala loved how Power and himself could have adult conversations. Waters sat back and listened to Wasala and Power talk about life, school, jokes, and miscellaneous subjects. Waters was secretly annoyed that they couldn't just hurry and get the dope. Wasala was always taking his sweet time. Wasala could sense Waters being impatient and was mad that Waters wasn't proud if his son. Power was so smart and polite, but Waters didn't care. Power should be in a private school, preparing to be a judge, but Waters paid no attention.

"Have you thought about what career you would like to pursue?" Wasala asked.

"I don't know. I like movies. Maybe I'll try to be a director."

"Allah has blessed you with intelligence Power. Never take Allah's blessing lightly. All that we have is only gifts from Allah, our eyesight, our ability to hear, our ability to breathe, everything. Allah has given you all of that, and much, much more Power. Respect your God and don't let it go to waste."

Power paused, "Yea. I am kinda' perfect, huh?"

Wasala and Power shared a laugh together.

Waters was annoyed that Wasala was taking so long he looked at Power and said.

"Power, Stop playing around. Everything's not a joke. Stop fuckin' around."

Power stopped laughing. Wasala looked at Waters and said.

Loyalty Is Blind

"Waters, my friend. There will be *no* swearing in my presence. You should listen to what I speak, for Allah has given you the greatest gift of all and you are least grateful."

Waters checked himself and shut up right in front of his own son. Wasala just wasn't the man to try. He had no problem taking a trip to go and see Allah. So you can guess how he felt about a disbeliever.

The limo stopped. Power looked out the window and seen a large mansion that looked like it could be a palace out of the movie *Aladdin*. This was one of Wasala's houses in America. One of the guards opened the limo door for them and walked them to the front door. They took their shoes off and walked inside. They went to a room with big chairs like thrones and they all sat. Wasala quickly waved his hand and one of the guards left the room to get the dope. Wasala and Power began to talk about the Qur'an. Wasala was extremely impressed that Power read the whole Qur'an. Power believed in God and considered himself Muslim, and Waters didn't even know. Wasala and Power's conversations were deep. Power would always learn a lot from Wasala in the short time he would spend with him. In the middle of their conversation someone politely interrupted them.

"Excuse me. Sorry for interrupting, but I need to talk to you real quick."

The voice came from the doorway. Wasala, Power, and Waters looked at who just spoke. He looked to be about 24, he was well built, he had the same copper tone as Wasala, and even shared some of the same features in the face as Wasala. His accent was very American and young. Not like Wasala's foreign but intelligent accent. He had short spiky hair, with a lined up mustache and beard. He was definitely a pretty boy.

"Hasad. I'll be finished in a minute," Wasala said with a tiny edge in his voice.

Hasad nodded and walked away. Power sensed Hasad was comfortable to act up around Wasala, and that he had a confident presence.

"That's your son?" Power asked.

Wasala let out a gentle laugh. "No Power. That is my nephew. Allah has blessed me with many, many things. Unfortunately, Allah did not want me to have a son I am infertile. I cannot create offspring."

"I deeply apologize."

"It's fine. I used to pray to Allah that I could have a son. It never happened. Allah does what he wills and I will always still appreciate Allah."

Power thought back to what Wasala said in the limo.

You should listen to what I speak. For Allah has given you the greatest gift of all and you are least grateful.

Now Power got it. He was honored that Wasala thought of him as a great gift from God. Power wished Waters would feel that way. He wondered if he looked at Hasad like a son.

"You are a very strong man Wasala. Where's Hasad's parents?"

"His mother is my sister. She passed away of cancer when Hasad was three and Hasad never knew his father."

"Do you look at Hasad like a son?"

Waters couldn't believe how deep their conversations have been. Wasala never spoke to Waters about the Qur'an or family. Waters always thought little Hasad was his son. He's been doing business with Wasala for years, and they never clicked like this.

Loyalty Is Blind

"No. Hasad is my nephew. I do pray he becomes less immature. He's so smart and skilled but he doesn't use his gifts. Everything he attempts, he completes. I'm proud of him, but I wish he submitted to Allah."

"Hasad's not Muslim?"

"No. Hasad has been in America since he was five. And this country of sin has taken my nephew's soul."

"Why didn't he move to Saudi Arabia, with you?"

"I don't want Hasad to resent Allah. I want him to accept Allah himself. That is why I will stay here for a few months of every year to teach my nephew."

"That's good. When you're here, can I come over and you could teach me?"

Wasala looked at Power in the eyes. He was so proud of him.

"It would be an honor to lead you to the path of Allah."

"Thank you Wasala. Can I bring my boys?"

"Of course, my friend, I would like to meet your friends."

Wasala and Power started to talk about Bills and Reign, and The Cipher. They talked about friendship and Wasala could tell that Power felt very strongly about his friends.

One of the body guards walked in with duffle bags full of dope.

"Your wait is over Waters. What you have awaited is here."

Waters grabbed the bags, and then looked at Wasala. "Thanks sir. I should be calling you soon."

"I'll see you my friend. As for you Power, take my number. Call me whenever you would like. I'll be in America for a while, so you can visit."

Power took Wasala's number.

Loyalty Is Blind

Chapter 9

"You say it looked like a palace from Aladdin?" Bills asked, excited.

"Yea, you know how rich people have themes for their mansions? Well his theme is like an Arabic theme mansion. He said we can visit whenever." Power said.

"We should get the dope straight from him. Shit, we could hit off Chino, instead of him givin' it to us," Reign suggested.

"Nah man, we gotta wait on that. I don't think he's ready to do business with me. Shit, I don't think we ready to do business wit' him."

"No doubt. You probably right."

***

Rome and Sylph walked through the Academy Homes parking lot at night holding hands heading to Sylph's apartment.

"Sup Sylph. I like them shades." Power said as they walked by.

Sylph didn't say anything to Power's comment. She acted like she didn't hear him. Rome had her in check like that. They walked pass The Cipher, up to Sylph's stoop, and into her apartment. Rome closed the door behind them, glared at Sylph, and said.

"The fuck was all that about?"

Sylph took a deep nervous breath. "Baby, What are you talking about?"

"You know what I'm talking about. You fucking that

Loyalty Is Blind

nigga Power? Why would he compliment you?"

"He wasn't complimenting me. He just liked my glasses," she cried

"Don't give me that bitch!" Rome yelled, so loud it made Sylph flinch.

"I promise. I only want you baby. I don't like no other man." Sylph said taking a step toward Rome and clutching his hand.

"Whatever." Rome snatched his hand back and waved her off. "Just hurry up and get a change of clothes for tomorrow. I don't wanna spend another second in this piece of shit projects."

"Okay baby, let me get washed up and we'll leave."

"Whatever, just hurry the hell up." Rome said, frustrated.

Sylph walked into her bathroom and looked in the mirror. She took off her glasses revealing a black eye that she has been hiding for a couple days.

What am I doing wrong? How do I make him trust me? What's wrong with me? Why can't I make him happy? She thought to herself, feeling guilty.

She rinsed off her face, put her glasses back on and packed a bag of clothes. She walked out into her living room and her and Rome left out of her front door. They walked through the parking lot where The Cipher was still sitting on Power's car.

"See you later Sylph." Power said as they were getting in Rome's car.

Sylph ignored Power.

When they got in the car and closed the doors Rome glared at Sylph. She knew that glare all too well. He did that whenever he was about to beat her. Sylph started to dread

Loyalty Is Blind

going over Rome's house because she knew what would happen. Sylph was starting to get fed up with it.

"What? Why are you mad at me?" Sylph spat.

"Bitch you know why. That nigga Power said something to you again. Why is he showing you so much attention?"

"I don't fuckin know? Maybe he's nice. Maybe he even thinks I' pretty. Why don't you ask him? Why do you only bring this up when we inside the house or in the car? You're quick to say something to me but I don't see you saying shit to him!" Sylph was letting all of her feelings out.

Rome actually was stumped. He had nothing to say, but he was still furious. He gritted his teeth.

"Bitch don't you-"

"And don't call me no bitch. You the bitch. You aint saying nothing to the nigga that's showing attention to your girl. You think I'm fucking Power? Well let's ask him." Sylph pushed the car door open as hard as she could and shot out of the car screaming.

"Power! Tell this nigga me and you don't fuck!"

"*Daaaaamn.*" Bills said, in a joking tone.

Power raised an eyebrow at Sylph. Rome got out of the car and yelled.

"Sylph get the fuck in the car!"

"No! You wanna accuse me of shit? You want proof? Ask him yourself!" Sylph yelled.

Rome honestly knew she wasn't fucking anyone. He simply was using a technique many abusers do. Just blame your girl for something you know she didn't do to constantly have her trying to gain your trust.

"Sylph, stop this shit and get in the car!" Rome said

"Why? So you can beat the shit out of me when we get to

Loyalty Is Blind

your house. You're quick to talk about every other nigga, and get on me when someone compliments me. Bitch ass nigga. You never talk to any other man like that but you talk crazy to me every day and night." Sylph said.

"Ch-ch-boom! Shots fired!" Bills yelled.

Rome gritted his teeth and glared at Sylph. She automatically regretted causing a scene.

"She said you a bitch nigga man." Bills instigated.

"Okay y'all get the fuck out of here with this bullshit." Power said. "And Rome, keep my damn name out of your mouth. Aint nobody fucking your girl. If I was hitting it, you wouldn't be hitting it."

"*Damn*, he said his dick game stronger than yours nigga!" Bills teased.

Rome was stuck in a tight spot that women beaters never want to get caught in. He was out on front street. He had to react to show his dominance or he would be just another weak nigga to Sylph and everyone else.

"Don't talk to me like that Power." Rome said trying to hide his fear.

Power laughed and said. "You chose your words wisely. You knew that was the toughest thing you could say to me without getting whooped on the spot. I'll talk to you any way I feel like. I aint one of these girls you be slapping around, and then pillow talking to them an hour later nigga. You a dumb ass nigga. You got your bitch walking around with shades on at night. I don't like seeing fake niggas come around The A. I ain't saying you fake cuz you slap bitches. Shit I slapped plenty of bitches, but I slap niggas too. You don't do that nigga. You a bitch who only pick on women."

Rome was embarrassed. Sylph looked at Power like he

Loyalty Is Blind

was crazy. She feared Rome. Rome always told her how tough he was. He was always talking about beating people up. Now she finally was seeing him on the spot.

Rome looked Power in the eyes. Power looked back at Rome like he was a nobody.

"You talk tough just because your boys are here." Rome said trying to hide his fear.

That was just about it to Power. He simply walked over to Rome and slapped him across his face like a bitch. The sound of the slap was so loud it bounced off of the walls of the projects.

Rome stumbled back holding his cheek. He looked Power in the eyes. Power glared back at Rome like he was ready to kill him. Rome took a step back, walked to his car, got in and drove away. Sylph watched the whole thing with a confused but amazed look on her face. Watching Rome get slapped she just felt like she watched a regular bullet kill Superman. Rome put so much fear into her but Power handled him like a bitch. She didn't know how to feel. Sylph slowly turned around and walked to her apartment

***

Sylph lay in her bed confused. She tried to sleep but she couldn't with her mind racing. She got out of bed and paced around her apartment in her pajama pants and tank top.

What if Rome comes back? He's crazy. He has a key. He can walk in at any moment and hurt me. He might kill me.

All of Sylph's thoughts made her eyes swell up in tears. She sat on her living room floor and rolled up in a ball, and buried her face in her knees as she cried. She didn't know what to do. She was somewhat relieved that it was over with

Loyalty Is Blind

Rome but she felt alone and scared. Every noise she heard at night she thought it was Rome coming back for her. She couldn't take all of the panicking. Rome put fear in her heart from all of the beatings.

She stood up and paced around the room again as she cried. She wiped the tears off of her face as she ran her hands through her hair. That's when she thought of Power. She was thankful that he helped her but he couldn't protect her now because she was alone in her apartment. Sylph's heart beat fast in fear. She didn't even think as she paced to her front door opened it, and walked out barefoot. She closed the door without even locking it behind her. She walked down her stoop and scurried across the silent parking lot. Her bare feet made quiet noises as they slapped the concrete. She hurried, not knowing if Rome was watching her from somewhere as she moved through the lights of the parking lot.

She rushed up to Power's apartment door and banged on it. She waited a moment and looked behind her hoping that Rome wasn't walking up behind her. She saw the coast was clear and knocked again. She was peeking over her shoulder again and jumped in fear when Power opened his door. She looked at Power standing there in his boxers with sleepy, tired eyes.

"What's up what you waking me up for?" Power asked, rubbing crust out of his eyes.

"I'm sorry Power. I literally am scared to death. I can't sleep. I think Rome is gonna come back and-"

"That nigga knows better than coming back here. Go home and get some sleep." Power interrupted Sylph, with a hint of irritation in his voice.

Power sounded sure that Rome wasn't coming back but

Sylph didn't feel so sure. She ran her hand through her hair as she nervously tapped her bare foot on Power's stoop. She took a shaky deep breath.

"Please. Can I just stay here tonight? I can barely breathe I'm so scared."

Power looked at Sylph with an annoyed look on his face. He sucked his teeth and sighed.

"Whatever. You can sleep on the damn couch," he said, opening the door wide and stepping back to let her in.

Sylph hurried in, walking pass Power. He shut the door behind him and looked at Sylph wearing her tank top that wasn't hiding anything under it. He looked her tight body up and down then shook away some thoughts almost all guys have when they are alone with a girl in a situation like this.

No way. This bitch is crazy. I aint even hit it and she already bringing me problems, Power thought.

Power shut the door, locked it and walked passed Sylph.

"You can sleep there," Power pointed to a leather couch. "I'll get you a pillow and blankets."

Sylph automatically felt relieved and her heartbeat slowed down. She took a deep breath and exhaled all of her worries as she sat down and sunk into the couch. She was already tired from worrying and pacing around so much. Power walked back in the room with a big comfy blanket and a fluffy pillow. He tossed them at her.

"Don't think you gonna be here every night. This is a one-time deal."

Power turned around and headed to his bedroom.

"Wait, Power." Power turned around and looked at Sylph, annoyed. "Uhm, thanks," she said

Power didn't say anything. He turned around and went

into his room, closing the door behind him. Sylph put the pillow on the arm of the couch, lied down and put the blanket over her body. She closed her eyes to rest as she smelled the sweet scent of Muslim oils of Power's home. She slowly drifted to sleep.

***

Sylph was awaken to a loud bang on the door. She sat up fast on. She almost forgot where she was. The bright sunlight beamed into the room and stung her eyes. Someone banged on the door again and Sylph heard someone's voice muffled through the closed door.

"Open up nigga!" Bills yelled.

Power woke up in his bed and tossed the blanket over his head.

"Damn open the damn door!" he yelled to Sylph, actually glad she was there so he didn't have to open it and listen to Bills bang on the door at 6:30 in the morning.

Sylph got off the couch, shuffled over to the door, unlocked it and opened it up while Bills was still knocking. She opened the door and Bills looked at her with a confused look on his face. His puzzled look quickly morphed into a smirk. Bills walked in, closed the door behind him and said.

"Damn, that was quick. He already hit that?"

Sylph's head jerked back at Bills' comment. "Wait-, no, we didn't-" she stuttered.

"That nigga got a little dick huh?" he joked.

Sylph rolled her eyes at Bills and sat back down on the couch.

Bills laughed at himself as he walked toward Power's room. Power sighed as he heard Bills coming near. He didn't

Loyalty Is Blind

feel like hearing Bills hassle him and joke this early in the morning.

Bills pushed Power's door open.

"My nigga," he laughed. "I knew it and on first night. You don't waste no time." He said, acting like Sylph wasn't in the next room and could hear every word.

"Shut your dumb ass up," Power said, tired.

Sylph decided she would go home. She wanted to thank Power but didn't know if now was the right time. She stood up off of the couch and looked toward Power's doorway where Bills was standing. She walked toward the door and peeked her head in.

"Uhm. Thanks Power. Really, I'm going back to my spot now."

Power didn't say anything. He just nodded his head up and down. Sylph walked toward the door, opened it, and that's when she noticed that she still didn't have shoes on. She didn't feel comfortable leaving without shoes in the daytime. She would look like a bum walking outside with no shoes in front of people. She closed the door and walked back toward Power's room.

"Sorry Power, but do you have any shoes or anything I can wear just to go home real quick? I didn't bring any shoes."

"Man, just use the slippers in front of the door." Power spat.

Sylph walked to the door, slipped on the slippers and walked outside. When Bills saw she closed the door, he said.

"You hit that?"

"Hell no," Power answered quickly.

"Soft ass nigga, playing the nice guy and shit. Trying to

save that pussy for later huh."

"No I ain't nigga. I ain't hittin' that. That bitch crazy. She just spazzed out on her man in front of us. All dramatic talking about she scared to sleep home alone. I can understand she scared and shit cuz that nigga used to beat her, but she way too crazy for me. She aint gonna be all on me sweatin' me. I won't let it happen."

***

The next day Sylph walked across the parking lot, holding Power's slippers in her hand. She wasn't so stressed out. She didn't think Rome would come for her in the daytime. He did still have a key to her house though. She was still worried about that. She had to change her locks. She walked up to Power's door and knocked. Power came to the door.

"Thanks," Sylph said with a smile, holding Power's slippers out to him.

Power took his slippers, and said, "No prob'."

He was about to shut the door until Sylph said, "Wait."

Power looked at her. "Sup?"

"Uhh, well, I kind of wanted to ask you if you could change my locks for me. I got a new lock and key. I just don't have tools and don't know how to do it anyways."

She looked at him for his reaction and answer. Power scrunched his face, like he was about to say no.

"Please. And I really wanna show you my appreciation, so I'll even cook you something to eat. Then after that I'll never bother you again."

"I'll help you." Power said, really not wanting this needy girl to beg him for stuff anymore.

Loyalty Is Blind

"Okay, thanks." Sylph chimed, all bubbly. "What do you want me to cook you?"

"Anything without pork. I'm Muslim."

Loyalty Is Blind

Chapter 10

Power was in Sylph's living room finishing up screwing in her knew door lock. Sylph was in the kitchen cooking up a meal for Power. Power twisted in the last screw on the lock.

"All done," he said as he walked to a couch and sat down.

He heard pots and pans clanging, grease bubbling and Sylph humming R&B songs to herself.

"I'm almost finished. Sit down at the table I'll bring you a plate." Sylph said, loud enough for Power to hear her.

"Yup."

He looked around her neat apartment then walked over and sat down at the table in the kitchen.

Sylph slid a delicious looking plate of food in front of Power. Mac and cheese, rice, fried chicken, with collard greens with smoked turkey cooked in them. Sylph went and grabbed herself a plate and sat down at the table across from him.

They ate and made small talk.

"So do you have a girlfriend?" Sylph asked.'

"Nope," Power said, already expecting her to ask that question, "No girl. I aint looking for one either. I'm too busy, and I don't got time for the bullshit."

Power could tell she was feeling him the way she's been giggling and flirting with him the whole dinner.

"That's good," Sylph said. "I understand. Nobody has time for the bullshit. But if you fuck with the right woman she doesn't bring you bullshit. She'll bring you happiness."

"Either way, I'm not trying to deal with anything. I don't got time to be chasing women or to be chased." Power said.

"Well I really appreciate you standing up for me against

Loyalty Is Blind

Rome, and letting me stay with you. That helped me more than you could know."

"Don't think nothing of it." Power waved her off. "It wasn't nothing. You're welcome though."

They finished the food.

Power stood up from the table. "Thanks for the meal. I have to head out now. Your new lock is set in. I wouldn't worry too much. That nigga Rome knows better than to come around here."

Sylph stood up and grabbed the dishes Power used. "Well thanks for fixing my lock. Stop by whenever. You know where I'm at."

Power was already on his way out her front door.

"Sure," he said, waving her off and closing her front door behind himself.

Sylph cleaned the dishes, walked into her room, got dressed in her pajamas, and laid on her comfy bed looking up at the ceiling. She still was stressed that Rome was going to come back and hurt her. She thought of Power again. She felt safe and protected around him. No other man has made her feel that way. She was in fear of Rome but Power handled Rome like a nobody. He was so confident that Rome wouldn't come back that it made her look at Power even more than she should. Sylph took a deep breath and pulled her blankets over her body. She cuddled into her blanket wishing she was back on Power's couch, instead of in a room where she has been beaten up by Rome in before. She took a deep breath as she tried to sleep throughout the night.

***

The next day Power was driving his Benz through his

Loyalty Is Blind

neighborhood. The sun was just coming down, as the new Jadakiss mixtape played out of his speakers. Power noticed a car has been behind him for a couple turns. Power wasn't too worried. It was a regular old Honda Civic If it was an unmarked police cruiser, he had nothing in his car. Power drove a down the street and turned down the back road. The car turned with him. That's when Power saw an all-white, unmarked moving truck pulling down the road. Power already knew what it was.

The jump out boys, he thought.

Power sped up, passed the truck, and turned left down a street that cut into the road near his projects. He took another turn, pulled into a random parking spot, took his keys out of the ignition, put them in his pocket, got out the car, closed the door, and ran across the street, cutting through another street. He ran as fast as he could, not seeing a sign of the truck or the car that followed him. He ran up to the fence around Academy Homes, climbed over it, and leaped to the ground inside. He ran up to his apartment and looked over his shoulder. He saw the truck pulling into the entrance of the projects. He fumbled for his keys in his pocket as the truck pulled into the parking lot. Power managed to get his key inside the lock and twisted as fast as he could. He opened the door and ran in his back room.

Power had nothing illegal in his apartment. The only thing he had was a bunch of money, which he had under his mattress. Power ran into his room and flipped the mattress over into the wall. Money scattered around the room from Power almost flipping the bed over. Power moved his eyes around the room, looking for something to put the money in. He saw a Northface backpack. He dashed over to the backpack, grabbed it and zipped it open. He grabbed hand fulls of the already counted money wrapped up in rubber bands as he tossed them in the bag, while breathing heavy and sweating. Power got most of the money in the bag when he heard the truck's engine coming from outside. His front door was still open and the police rushed in. Power quickly ran over to his window, slid it open, tossed the backpack out, climbed out the window, and dropped to the ground.

    He had to think fast. Power looked around. He was now in the back of his apartment, which was basically a grassy area that had other apartments. Power didn't want to walk into any yard or open areas. He really had nowhere to go. He looked to the right in a panic and he could see the back of Sylph's apartment. He ran over to her window as he held the backpack by both straps in his right hand. He banged on her back window as hard as he could without breaking it. It felt like it took Sylph forever to slide the window open with a puzzled look on her face.

    "Power?" she looked worried and confused. "What happened? Are you-"

    Power didn't even listen to her. He pushed the backpack into her window and said,

    "Take this and hide it. Don't open it," he said, and then ran off.

    Power could have jumped into Sylph's window and hide in there, but he didn't want any police dogs to track his scent. He didn't want to get caught with the money. His best bet was to simply run and let the police catch him when he had nothing on him. Power ran around a corner when he was tackled by a cop in plain clothes with a badge dangling from a chain on his neck. Two other cops followed and helped the officer restrain and handcuff Power. They made sure to punch and kick Power in the ribs a few times.

***

Power sat in an interrogation room alone. He sat in a wobbly steel chair with an old, dirty, scarred, dingy, metal table in front of it. An empty chair sat directly across from him. A bright light beamed on him from a ceiling. Power remained calm. He assumed the police searched his house and the whole area around his projects but he knew that they would find nothing. He wasn't worried about that. He was worried about Sylph though. He just left her with a lot of money and didn't trust her at all. She was his only option at the time. He couldn't go to Bills' or Reign's apartments because they were across from his apartment and not on the same side of his. Power sighed as he tried to look and be calm in front of the camera's pointing at him from the corners of the ceiling.

A cop walked into the room holding a folder with some papers in it. The cop sat down in the empty chair and opened the folder up, all the while looking at Power for a reaction, which he saw none. Power knew he could ask for a lawyer but was confident that they had nothing on him. He also wanted to see if he could get information out of the situation as to why they were even following him.

The cop leaned over closer to Power. "We know everything. You might as well confess here. It will only make things easier." His accent was heavy Boston.

Power looked at the officer like he had no idea what he was talking about.

"Sir I have no idea what you are talking about."

Loyalty Is Blind

"Tough nut huh?" the cop laughed. "Then why would you run?"

"I'm sorry I ran," Power lied. "It was a regular Civic following me. I didn't know it was a cop following me. I thought it was a murderer or some gang bangers or something." Power was being sarcastic.

"You think I'm dumb?" the cop stood up. "I got all the evidence I need on you. You better help yourself and cooperate or all the blames going on you!"

Power sat back and raised his hands like he was scared.

"Please sir. I have no idea what you're talking about."

The cop was frustrated. He could tell Power wasn't going to crack. He shook his head.

"Well, you're under arrest anyway buddy."

"For what?" Power laughed.

"Let's start with resisting arrest, disorderly conduct, disturbing the peace, abandoning a vehicle, assault and battery on a police officer, intimidating a witness."

Power sat back in his chair. The police threw in a couple charges just to hassle Power.

"I want my fuckin' lawyer you piece of shit." Power said angry.

The cop laughed at him and walked out of the interrogation room.

***

Power was trying to sleep in the holding cell. He was arrested at around 7:30 on a Saturday evening. The police held him with no bail so he had to wait until Monday to go to court. He didn't want to call Bills or Reign because he felt that would make the police watch them. He sat in his cell worried about his money.

I can kiss that money bye, bye. He thought, mad at himself for not being more careful.

The day came where Power had to go to court. Power had already called his lawyer and planned on meeting him at courthouse. The police woke power up, cuffed him, shackled him, chained him to some other men who had to go to court who were drunks, wife beaters and petty criminals, and then shipped them to court in a van. The police took them out of the van and took them into the courtroom from the back and into the holding cells before they took their shoes off. Power's lawyer, Kaleb Babinski walked up to Power's cell he leaned in close to the bars to talk to Power face to face.

"So what's the deal?" Power asked.

Kaleb put on his reading glasses. "The deal is, it's all bullshit. They made a case out of absolutely nothing."

"But why? Why they on me?" Power asked.

"No idea," Kaleb shrugged "My guess would be some drug user or some young man got arrested and mentioned your name for something. The police tried to arrest you and scare you to get you to flip. They think you're into something so they're gonna hassle you and fuck with you a little. They're trying to get you to tell on something."

"So what do I do"

"Honestly, I've seen this many times. The DA and the police are working very close on this one, along with the judge. They think you're an impact player with no type of proof, so they will try and give you a little bit of time knowing the charges won't stick. They'll put your bail to a couple hundred thousand and if you post it they will be on you even more."

Loyalty Is Blind

"Damn," Power said, as he thought.

He didn't care about doing jail time. No man should fear jail time if they are doing illegal business. He was worried about his money. Sylph would definitely know it was money in the bag and she would spend it. Power knew she had a little crush on him but he was positive that the money was worth way more than her little crush.

Kaleb and Power talked a little more. Kaleb told Power that he would get a high bail and that the DA had a fake story from the police and there wasn't much he could do until later on. Kaleb went into the courtroom.

Power felt like he waited in that cell forever until they called his name. A bailiff led Power to the courtroom. Power walked in, he scanned the room looking for anyone he knew. That's when he saw Sylph sitting on one of the benches dressed up nice like she was going on a job interview. Sylph smiled at Power, like she was happy to see he was okay. Power smiled back because he was happy that she wasn't somewhere spending his money.

Power was lead to stand in front of the judge in cuffs, with no shoes on, just socks. Kaleb spoke for Power. He tried his best to make Power look squeaky clean. Kaleb was a good slick talking lawyer and he did a good job. Then the DA spoke.

"Your honor, the defendant was speeding down Washington street when an officer in a marked police vehicle flashed his sirens to pull him over for a routine traffic stop. The defendant then resisted arrest by turning onto Townsend street, stopped his car in the middle of the road and fled on foot. He then proceeded to jump a fence, running into Academy Homes Projects, a place know for crime and drug activity. He ran to an apartment listed in the police database as his address, and then fled out the back door. Police attempted to apprehend him but he punched an officer in the face. The officers managed to cuff him and asked him why he ran, he then threatened the officer by saying, quote on quote, *I am going to kill you*, end quote. He was then arrested and booked."

Power expected the DA to say a police report full of lies. He wasn't surprised. The DA always did that to everyone. The judge put a continuance on Power's hearing and held him without bail like his lawyer said he would. The bailiffs then took Power and lead him back down to the cells. Power waited for about a half hour before Kaleb came back down.

"Sorry, Power." Kaleb said, "but the judge, DA, and police are all in this together. This happens from time to time. Don't worry though, I'll beat the shit out of this case and you'll be out at your next court date which is in a month. They have nothing on you."

"I'm not worried about it. Thanks for coming. I'll see you in a month." Power said.

"And oh ya. I talked to your girlfriend."

Power snapped his head back. "My girlfriend?"

"Ya. Sylph she said her name was."

"What did she say?"

"She wanted me to ask you what did you want her to do with your backpack."

"Tell her I said thanks, and give it to one of the other two."

"Gotcha." Kaleb said, already fully aware that Power was talking about Reign and Bills.

Loyalty Is Blind

Loyalty Is Blind

Chapter 11

Sylph sat on her bed in her room staring at Power's backpack in the corner. She didn't know what to do. Power had just gave her the backpack through her window. He looked like he was worried so she wondered what was in the bag. She didn't want any drugs or guns in her apartment. She walked over to the bag and zipped it. Her heart skipped a beat and her jaw dropped as she looked at more money than she's ever seen in her life. She slowly zipped the bag closed and walked back over to her bed laying down on it sideways as she thought.

What is he doing with that kind of money? Does he really trusts me with his money?

Sylph then sat up in her bed quickly. *He trusts me,* she smiled to herself.

Not only did she feel protected around Power, but he trusted her with all of this money. In Sylph's mind, that showed that he had some type of feelings for her. Sylph bounced around the bed smiling to herself as she thought of Power.

He's trusting me with something very important. He could have went to Bills or Reign but he came to me. That shows that he put me on the same level as his two best friends.

***

Power's court date came. Sylph waited in the courtroom since nine o'clock. She sat in her nice suit, which was dressy and classy. She sat on one of the dirty benches of the courtroom with marks and carvings on every inch of the back. Police, lawyers, and other court officials walked

Loyalty Is Blind

around working. Sylph watched a bunch of people stand in front of the judge and be put in jail. Only 2 or 3 times did she see people get off for petty crimes. Then Power was lead into the courtroom in handcuffs. Sylph smiled at him and Power smiled back. Her heart skipped a beat.

He's happy to see me. He's happy that I'm here to support him.

She heard the DA's bullshit story and didn't even question that it was all lies. Everyone from Boston knew how the court system worked. It was nothing new to Sylph. Power's lawyer stepped up and spoke for him but he wasn't very effective against the DA and judge's planned attack. After they took Power downstairs Sylph quietly walked over to Power's lawyer and tapped him on the shoulder.

"Excuse me," Sylph whispered trying to be quiet in court. "I'm Sylph, Power's girlfriend. Can I please talk to you in the lobby?"

"Of course," Kaleb said, following her out of the courtroom.

"Can you please go ask Power a question for me?"

"Sure, what is it?" Kaleb asked.

"Just ask him what he wants me to do with his backpack."

"Okay, I wasn't aware he had a girlfriend but I'll talk to him."

"Thank you sir. I'll be waiting her."

Sylph waited for a while until Kaleb came back in the lobby.

"Give it to Bills or Reign."

Sylph nodded her head and walked out of the courthouse.

***

Loyalty Is Blind

Power walked down the unit in the maximum security county jail. He carried a plastic green box as he wore an orange jump suit. He walked down the jail isle with two tiers going up on one side. Each door was thick steel with a long skinny window. Stale air filled the jail and no sunlight could be seen in the large concrete unit with no windows. Four seated tables were built into the clean white tiled floors. Power looked up at the inmates looking down at him from the tiers above. A couple people knew Power from his reputation and Power recognized a couple of people. Power had a plan. He would simply keep to himself. He didn't come in to make any friends. Power walked to his assigned cell, where he saw a young man lying on the bottom bunk, listening to his radio. When he saw Power walk in he sat up in the bunk and took the ear buds out of his ears.

"Sup fam, I'm Lo."

"I'm Power," he introduced himself as he slid his box under the bunk.

***

Sylph knocked on Reign's door, still in her court clothes. Reign opened his door.

"Sup?" Reign said, not sure of why she was there.

"Power left something with me to give you."

"Where at?" Reign asked.

"At my apartment, so c'mon."

Reign followed Sylph to her apartment. They walked through the front door and Sylph told Reign to take a seat. Reign sat there for a few seconds as Sylph walked to her room, grabbed the bag, and brought it out to him. He unzipped the bag and looked at the money with a blank look

Loyalty Is Blind

on his face. Sylph would have never suspected Reign to be as surprised as he really was inside. Reign was good at hiding his emotions. Reign zipped the bag closed, and then looked at Sylph.

"So exactly what is going on?"

"All I know is Power was running from the police. He came to my bedroom window and handed me that backpack. He told me to hide it and keep it safe so I did. He got arrested, and had court today. They held him with no bail and his court date is in a couple months. His lawyer directed me to give that to you or Bills."

Reign assumed that Power only had her hold it because he had no other choice. Sylph thought otherwise. Reign was still surprised Sylph didn't steal the money or spend any of it. Reign unzipped the bag again and pulled out a wad of cash.

"Here, take this money for your troubles."

"I don't want it." Sylph said, shaking her head as she waved her hand in front of her, "I don't need to be paid. I hold it down for my people for free."

"You don't have to tell me twice." Reign shrugged as he put the money back in the backpack. "I just wanna say that's loyal. Power will appreciate that. I appreciate that. We need more real people like you around. You could have done something shady when Power got bagged, and you didn't. Good lookin' out."

Sylph felt gassed that Reign said that.

"Power's a good guy. He held me down, so I'll hold him down. I'm about to write him tonight and try and visit him soon"

Reign stood up. "Well thanks. He'll appreciate it. I talked to his lawyer already. He should be good with his case. I'm

gonna head out of here though."
Reign left with the backpack.

***

A couple days had passed. Power was doing pushups in his cell when Lo walked in.

"The C.O got some mail for you at the front desk, fam."

Power stood up from the floor, walked out of his cell, and to the C.O's desk. He told the C.O his ID number and the C.O handed him an already opened letter with scotch tape holding it shut. Power looked at the envelope and saw it was from Sylph. Power caught himself smiling. There was something about getting letters in jail that makes you happy. Power walked to his cell, jumped on his bunk, lay down, opened his, letter, and read it.

Hey Power,

How have you been? I hope you're okay. I gave Reign your backpack. Sorry I lied to your lawyer and told him I was your gf, but I wanted him to trust me and take time to talk to me. Reign said everything should be good with your case so I'm happy about that :) I left my number at the top of the letter. Call me as soon as you can! I miss you. Bills told me to tell you don't drop the soap. The police left your house a mess, don't worry, Reign has a key, he locked your door. Do you want me to clean your house for you? I want everything to be nice and clean for when you get out. I don't want to have to worry about anything while you're in or when you get out. Well I'm gonna head out now. Write and call me every day! Miss you.
    Love Sylph

Loyalty Is Blind

Power folded up the letter, put it back in the envelope. He slid the envelope under his bunk, laid down and looked at the ceiling. Sylph's letter helped relieve some of his jail stress. He couldn't wait to write her back and talk to her on the phone. Power had no feelings for Sylph, he was just happy to keep in touch with anyone on the streets.

***

Sylph sat on her couch reading a book when her phone rang. She picked her phone up off her couch and answered.

"Hello"

An automated voice spoke. "You have a collect call from *Power.*"

Sylph's heart skipped a beat when she heard Power's voice over the phone.

Sylph jumped out of her seat and dropped her book on the ground. Her heat beat faster as she jumped up and down like a little kid on Christmas.

The automated voice continued, "An inmate at Nashua Street Jail. This phone call is subject to monitoring and recording. To accept charges, press 1. To refuse call, press 2. To block all calls from this facility, press 3."

Sylph wasted no time to press 1. The phone was silent for a couple seconds until she heard Power's voice.

"Hello."

"Hey Power," she said trying not to sound as excited as she was, "How you been?"

"I been maintaining. I'm taking this day by day."

They made small talk and caught up with each other. Sylph was smiling the whole time.

Loyalty Is Blind

"How have you been sleeping at your own apartment? It's hard to sleep when it aint my couch huh?" Power joked.

"It's not that bad." Sylph lied. "I know he's not coming back, but it's still kind of scary."

"Well if you want you can stay at my house until I get out. I need someone to clean it and watch over it."

Sylph was gassed up. Whenever Power asked her to do something it made her feel important. She was used to Rome commanding her to do pointless things. When Power asked her to do something that actually mattered to him, she felt like she mattered, like she was important that she was entrusted with something. She felt like Power trusted her with his house and money. She never felt like Rome trusted her. She felt like her loyalty was finally being recognized by Power.

"I'll clean it up and watch over it for you." Sylph said, excited.

An automated voice spoke.

"You have 60 seconds until this phone call ends."

Sylph dreaded that automated voice.

"Well I should be heading out," Power said, "Get my key from Reign. Clean up the apartment and stay there if you want. I'll write you back and maybe I'll call you in a couple days or something."

"Okay, call me whenever. I miss you. Hold your head up hun." Sylph said, sad that the half hour phone call was so short.

The phone call was disconnected. Sylph sighed. She felt like a little girl with a crush in middle school. She smiled as she thought about her phone conversation.

Loyalty Is Blind

***

Sylph and Power talked on the phone at least twice a week. Sylph was falling hard for Power. She couldn't wait for him to come home. Power stayed getting letters, pictures, and even a couple visits. Finally, Power's court date came. Kaleb fought the case and got it dismissed. Sylph was at the jail waiting for them to release Power. Sylph sat on the hood of her car in the jail parking lot. She saw Power come out the front door of the jail and walk onto the front steps carrying what looked like a laundry bag over his shoulder. Sylph stood up and waved to Power with a smile. Power waved back as he walked down the steps. He made his way across the parking lot. Sylph ran up to him and hugged him tight. Power hugged her back as he laughed.

Sylph pulled back from him. "You look great! How does it feel?"

"It feels good. I'm hungry as hell though." Power said clenching his stomach.

"Let's go to your apartment. I'll cook you something."

They got into Sylph's car and drove to Power's Academy Homes. Sylph had the new Styles P mixtape playing through her speakers. She knew Power could only listen to this type of music. He hated the music on the radio so she got him the new mixtape so he could hear something he actually liked. They went to Power's apartment and Sylph cooked him a big meal and they talked.

"So have you ever been in love?" Sylph asked.

Power shrugged and asked, "What you mean?"

"C'mon, you know what I mean."

"Not really." Power shook his head. "I mean. Not the type of love you're thinking."

Loyalty Is Blind

Sylph ticked her head to the side, and asked, "What do you mean?"

"It's like this." Power dropped his fork on his plate, and leaned closer to Sylph. "You tell me. Did you love Rome?"

Sylph looked down at her plate of food and moved the food around with her fork.

"I did love him-"

"No. You didn't love him. You might have thought you loved him, you might have felt like you loved him, but love is eternal, it is before and after anything that happens between two people."

Sylph looked into Power's eyes and let him continue.

"I love my niggas Reign and Bills. I always will. I don't think there is anyone else in the world as loyal as them two. If you loyal to someone, that's the best way to show them you love them. Just because you want to be with someone doesn't mean you love them. Love goes both ways. If Rome loved you he would never put his hands on you. It's impossible to love someone who doesn't love you just as much. If you believe that love is only strong feelings for someone, then you really have no idea what love is. I think you're a real ass person, a loyal ass person. I can tell you that I got mad love for you but that don't mean I wanna be your man or anything. Love has nothing to do with relationships to me. It's all about family in my opinion."

Sylph respected what Power was saying but she wanted to be his woman, not his friend.

She said, "Well I'm loyal to you. Does that mean I love you too?"

Power laughed and said. "Sylph, we both got love for each other. Aint nothing wrong with that. You got a lot of

Loyalty Is Blind

questions about love. That might have to be your new name. Love," Power laughed.

"Sounds good to me." Sylph smiled. "But I'm gonna be real Power. I like you. I think you're everything I ever wanted in a man. It sounds like you just wanna be my friend, and that's not what I want. I want you to give me a chance to be your girl."

"Love, I lost my mom young." Power said and paused. "She was perfect. It sucks cuz she died for some shit my father was into. So I promised myself I would never bring no woman I got love for into no shit I'm into. Maybe when I'm ready to chill out and get out the game we can try something between us. I appreciate everything you've done for me and I do like you but I can't do it. Not when I saw my mom die over this shit."

"Power, I don't care if you hustling, or working, or whatever. I wanna ride wit' you. Just let me show you."

Power shook his head, and said, "Nah Love. Sorry, I can't. I got love for you and I like you but it aint like that right now. Let's just be good friends. It's better that way.

Sylph didn't even hear half of the shit Power said. All she heard Power say was he had love for her and he liked her. The rest of the shit Power said wasn't anything to her. As far as she was concerned she would be the perfect woman for Power and make him be with her, make him not care that he was in the game because she sure as hell didn't care. Everything about Power made Sylph go crazy inside. Sylph stood up and walked right up to Power. She pushed him back into his seat and straddled him.

"Sylph. What are you doing?" Power said. "I thought I told you-"

Loyalty Is Blind

Sylph cut him off with a kiss on the lips. She kissed him as passionately as she could.

"Shut up. I want you. I don't care what you say. I'll be the perfect woman for you," she continued to kiss him.

Power kissed her back, he couldn't help himself. Being in jail for those two months made him way to in need of attention from a woman. Sylph kissed on his cheek then licked and sucked on his neck. She lifted his shirt over his head and kissed down his chest. She got on her knees in front of him as she kissed all the way down from his chest, to his waste.

"You already the perfect man for me. I can be the perfect girl for you." she said as she undid his belt.

Power couldn't say anything. He was in too deep. He hasn't felt a woman's touch in months. Sylph pulled Power's dick out and took him into her mouth. She started to suck on him as she moved her tongue around in her mouth and moaned like she loved the taste of him. She took her mouth off of his dick and her lips popped from her sucking so hard, and she said.

"I'll take good care of you, every night before you go to bed and every morning when you wake up."

She took him into her mouth as she kept eye contact with him and deep throated his whole dick. She started to bob her head up and down in a rhythm as she held onto his dick with her hand. She started to stroke him with her hand as she sucked, moaned and bobbed, jacking him off as she was going to work. She then started to twist her head and twisted both hands on his shaft as she blew him away. Power was loving it.

He felt like he was ready to explode in her mouth. Sylph

Loyalty Is Blind

kept eye contact with him the whole time. She then took one of her hands, grabbed him by his wrist, and placed his hand on the back of her own head. Power pushed her head down, getting his dick all the way down her throat. Sylph didn't even blink as she took it all. Power grabbed a handful of her curly hair as she bobbed away faster and faster. Power could feel his nut coming. He leaned back in his chair as she moaned louder. She could tell Power was about to come so she sucked harder, bobbed faster and moaned loader.

"I'm about to nut." Power warned her as he looked in her eyes while she sucked him off.

She just kept staring at him as she bobbed her head up and down his dick. Power started to nut in her mouth. Sylph took him deep down her throat and swallowed every drop. Power held onto the back of her head tight.

"Damn, Sylph." he said out of breath.

Sylph's lips smacked when she took Power's dick out of her mouth. She wiped her mouth with the back of her hand, stood up and said.

"Don't worry Power. I'll give you time to warm up to me."

Power pulled his pants up and said.

"Well, thanks for hookin me up. But I'm keeping it real wit you. I ain't lookin for no relationship."

Sylph waved him off and said.

"You'll change your mind soon."

Loyalty Is Blind

Chapter 12

The next month, The Cipher spent a weekend at Wasala's mansion. Wasala taught Power about Islam and the Qur'an. He taught him about Zakat, Salat, and all the basics. Power began to really take the Muslim religion seriously. Power would pray for his mother to be accepted into paradise, every chance he got. He felt his mother would be very proud of him, and he knew in his heart he would see her again. Bills and Reign got to know Hasad. Hasad seemed to be very smart, and still tough. He connected with Reign. Hasad was trained by the body guards and wanted to be an enforcer for Wasala eventually.

Wasala was reciting a verse from the Qur'an, to Power, when he got a call on his big mobile phone. Wasala answered.

"Hello."

"Wasala! I'm at my safe house! They breakin' in right now! I'm shot!" Waters yelled.

Power could hear Waters, but couldn't make out what he was saying. He stood up, and asked, "Is he a'ight?" Power asked. His eyebrows drew inward and he sounded pretty nervous.

Wasala gave Power an uncomfortable look.

"Slow down Waters. Explain what is happening. Who is after you?"

"They all in masks! I don't know who they are, but they gonna kill me!" Waters shouted in the phone.

Gunshots could be heard in the background.

"We are on our way," Wasala said sternly.

The Cipher and Wasala were quickly escorted to the limo, followed by three cars, full of skilled body guards. The

Loyalty Is Blind

ride felt like it took forever. Eventually, they came up to Waters' house. The front door was wide opened. The Cipher and Wasala rushed in, tightly protected by Wasala's professional security. Wasala's security moved as a unit using hand signs to communicate with each other as they moved into the house on by one. When they cleared each room they gave the okay for Wasala and The Cipher to come inside. Power looked around the house for a couple painstaking seconds. He saw the house was ransacked. He saw tables turned over and couches ripped open, and seen his father's dead body bled out on the floor. Power walked toward his father's dead body with bullet holes in his chest, lying in a puddle of blood.

Power looked into his father's dead opened eyes, staring back into nothingness. He crouched down next to his dead father and shed a tear. Bills and Reign watched their friend in agony. Wasala put his hand on Power's shoulder. Power looked up at Wasala, and asked him the same question that he asked his father when he found his mother.

He looked into Wasala's eyes and asked. "Why?"

"Power. This is a test from Allah. Maybe Allah doesn't see fit for Waters to be in your life anymore. Allah does what he wills. But I do promise, it will get better if you show faith."

That answer was a lot deeper then what Waters answered. Power thought back.

It's life son.

"We must go now before the authorities arrive," Wasala said.

***

They all went back to Wasala's house. Power prayed for his father. He had no idea what he would do. Wasala offered help, money, a place to stay, but Power politely refused. The next day, the cops went to Power's home in Academy Homes and tore shit up from the ceiling to the floor. They took all the money in the house for their *investigation*. Now Power had nothing, not even a home. The Cipher was at Sylph's house, shocked at everything that's been happening. Sylph felt pain for Power. She really wanted to help him. She would do anything in the world for him. Anything Power asked for, Sylph would do. Her heart ached for him.

"I'm sorry that you gotta go through all this shit my nigga. What should we do?" Bills asked.

"I don't know man. I got no money, no home. Nothing." Power said.

"I say we find out who it was and kill these niggas," Reign said.

"I don't know. I'm just fucked up right now," Power said in a weak tone.

He sounded like he could cry.

A tear fell down Sylph's cheek, she began to sob. She walked up to Power and hugged him tightly, then cried in his arms.

"I'm so sorry. You don't deserve this, Power," Sylph said, between cries.

Power hugged Sylph tight, but gently. Their hearts beat together. Power held back tears as he took a deep breath. Bills and Reign joined the hug. They all held each other.

"My brotha, we gon' get these niggas, on dogs," Reign said.

They hugged, then Power stepped back, and they

separated.

Power wiped away Sylph's tears gently with his hand, then said.

"I'll be a'ight. Allah's testing me."

Sylph sniffled.

"Where you gonna stay tonight?" Bills asked.

Power did a weak shrug. He didn't know where he would stay.

"Stay here tonight," Sylph said with tear filled eyes.

"No, just stay at my crib." Bills said.

"Shut up Bills," Sylph said glaring at him.

Bills jerked his head back, looking at Sylph, and said.

"Damn killa, chill out." Bills said.

Sylph looked back at Power, and said, "You can sleep on my bed. I'll give you your space and sleep on the couch.

Power rubbed his head, and then said, "Yeah. I'll just sleep in your room I guess."

"Well get some sleep," Reign said, with a nod. "Because later we gotta meet Chino and-"

"Chill," Power said cutting off Reign. "Not around Sylph."

"Come on nigga. I understand you're stressed right now but Sylph rides wit' us nigga. Cut her some slack and stop treating her like a baby." Reign proudly said.

The room was silent.

"But whatever man," Reign said. "You need some rest. Sleep it off, then we'll be on our way.

**

Power laid in Sylph's bed. Sylph's room was neat and organized. She had a white desk with a mirror in the corner with pictures of Reign, Bills, Power and herself plastered all over the bottom of it. She had quotes she liked written on the mirror. Her room was painted a girly light pink color. Her dresser sat at the front of the room with her flat screen TV on it. He was grateful for being able to sleep under a roof. Power thought about his father and mother, he couldn't sleep, he could barely breathe. Sylph laid on her couch and silently cried to herself. Power's heart was in pain, he had a lump in his throat. He prayed for his father's forgiveness.

Allah, why? Power thought.

Allah didn't answer him.

He clenched his eyes shut, and thought.

Allah, please help me. Somehow, I just need help.

Sylph got up off of the couch, walked toward her door in her pajamas and peeked into her bedroom. She looked at Power, he was dimly lit up by the shine of the street light beaming into her window. She couldn't take the sight of him in pain. She walked to him, and carefully pulled the blanket off of his head. As the sheet slowly went down Power's face, he saw Sylph's beautiful face, shining from the street light.

He felt like Allah answered him.

Sylph moved the blanket to the side so she could lay next to him.

Power thought about it, then said, "Sylph, nah, I just can't."

"Shhh," Sylph said, as tears still dropped.

She gently laid next to him and pulled the covers up. She buried her face in his chest, and cried. A tear fell from Power's eye, they cried together. Power's body was weak. Power pressed his face in the pillow, crying, as Sylph rubbed his back. Power became calm, he was comfortable in the bed, next to Sylph. She moved his arm to cuddle in close with him, but he didn't move his arm.

"Love, chill out," Power said.

"Please Power. Stop running from me," Sylph pleaded.

Power moved his arm and pulled Sylph closer into himself. They hugged as their faces touched. They both slowly calmed down and stopped crying.

"What you cryin for?" Power asked.

Sylph looked into Power's eyes, then said, "Your pain is my pain."

Power understood her. They were on a level to feel each other's pain.

They were silent.

I love you. Power thought.

Sylph softly rubbed his cheek, then held his cheek in her palms and gently pulled his face toward hers. Power thought about pulling back. Nervousness attacked again. But suddenly, it happened. They kissed. They both shared their first kiss. Power felt like everything would be fine as he kissed her. Sylph felt safe. She felt like she was floating on a warm cloud. Power felt right, but wrong at the same time. He couldn't be with Sylph, he would only ruin her life. But he needed her right now. They drifted off into sleep.

Chapter 13

Power laid in Sylph's bed. He's been asleep all day, he just didn't have it in him to get up yet. He heard Sylph walk in the room. She gently pushed his shoulder. Power turned around to look at Sylph. He almost got whip lash at the sight of her. She was all done up. She was on point.

Damn you sexy. He thought.

Knowing his mind entered a forbidden territory, he backed off and said.

"Wussup?" his voice barely covered his amazement.

"How you doin'?"

"I'm just kinda tired. I'm fine though."

Sylph went to lay down next to him. Power stopped her.

"I just wanna lay alone for a little while."

Just take it slow. You got forever to be with him. She thought to herself

Sylph didn't want to smother Power. She would give him time to get comfortable.

"Aight Power. I'll be here if you need me," she said, then walked away.

Power wished he could just force himself to give his all to Sylph, and push his insecurities and doubts aside, but he couldn't do it. Sylph left the room and Power faded off to sleep.

Power was awoken, that night, to Sylph silently watching him sleep. She looked beautiful in the dim moonlight. He felt a lot better, thanks to all of the rest.

"Get up. Bills and Reign are on the way," Sylph gently whispered.

Loyalty Is Blind

He stood up and stretched out. He had a new edge, he was ready. Sylph's bedroom door shot open and Reign stuck his head in. Reign shifted his cautious gaze left and right, and then looked at Power. He noticed Power was up and ready, then he gave Power a proud smile. Power returned a smile, with a look like *I'm a'ight.*

Reign nodded at Power, then said. "C'mon nigga. Chino's waitin'."

Power started to walk to the door.

Sylph put her hand on his shoulder then asked.

"Want me to give you a ride?"

"Nah Love. Stay here. I'll be back tonight."

Sylph's heart jumped at Power's words. He's coming back home to her. She couldn't wait to lay with him all night. She wouldn't sleep one wink until he was back home safely.

"Okay, be careful," she said as she hugged him.

Power held Sylph.

"Love?" Bills shouted from the living room. "That's Sylph's name now? Reign, Tell them damn love birds to hurry the fuck up!" Bills loudly yelled from Sylph's living room.

Power slowly stepped back from Sylph, looked at Reign, and said, "Tell that skinny ass nigga to shut his mouth before I beat his little ass."

Reign sighed as he shook his head.

"Get your punk ass out here and say that shit to my face."

Power walked toward Sylph's door, Reign moved out the way and Power walked out, then dashed at Bills.

"Reign," Sylph said, getting his attention.

"Sup Love?"

"Make sure Power comes home safe."

Loyalty Is Blind

"What are you his moms?"

Sylph thought for a second, then said. "Is that really what it sounds like?"

"Yea. You gotta be tough and confident Love. That whole *be careful* shit is plain corny."

Sylph could hear Bills and Power wrestling in the living room.

"I don't wanna sound like that."

Sylph heard a thud, followed by Power's laugh.

"I never thought of it like that. Thanks Reign."

"No problem Love." Reign said.

Sylph heard Bills yell *hi yah*, then Power grunt in pain like *ugh!* She gasped, pushed Reign out the way and stuck her head out the door. She seen Bills had Power in a head lock.

"Bills! Get off of him!"

Reign sucked his teeth at the drama queen.

Bills looked at Sylph as he held Power in a head lock.

"Say another word, and I'll snap his neck," Bills said playfully.

Sylph covered her mouth and giggled. Bills pushed Power away from himself and said. "I'm lettin you live cuz Love begged for your life nigga."

Bills looked at Sylph and gave her his half smile and wink.

Sylph winked back.

"Whatever nigga, let's go, we wastin time," Power said.

"Power will be back tonight," Reign said as they walked off.

"I'll be waitin," Sylph said.

Loyalty Is Blind

Chapter 14

The Cipher walked into Chino's house and Chino was sitting on the sofa.

"Sup Power? You a'ight homie?" Chino asked.

"I'm good my nigga," Power said as he gave Chino dap with the threes.

"So wassup Chino?" Reign asked.

"Shit got all fucked up since Waters died. Waters was the man hittin off my connect. Now my connect aint got shit."

"Damn. So now since you aint got shit, we aint gon get shit," Bills said, disappointed.

"Yea nigga, but that aint even the issue right now. I called y'all here cuz I found out who killed Waters."

"Who?" Power growled, with bloodlust in his voice.

"These niggas yo' papa was doin business wit. No disrespect, but yo papa was fuckin' with alotta niggas money right before he died. He just happened to fuck wit the wrong people this time."

"That can't be right. Why would Waters fuck up another niggas money. He wasn't broke, he didn't have to take from no one," Bills said in disbelief.

"Waters just wasn't bringing in money like he used to. The thing about Waters was he always had a steady price for years and years. Then this OG pimp nigga, Sammy Smooth, came round and was sellin' the shit for lower."

"Why didn't Waters just take out Sammy Smooth?" Reign asked.

"Cuz Sammy Smooth was gettin his dope from the same connect that Waters was. He didn't want beef with his own connect."

Wasala, Power thought.

Loyalty Is Blind

"I get it. He didn't wanna get in his own connects way. But how come Waters didn't just drop the price?" Bills asked.

"My pops got too much pride. I could really see my pops just taking niggas money before dropping a price," Power explained.

"So who took out Waters?" Reign asked.

"One of them Eastside cats. This brotha' named Bigz."

"Damn, them East Side niggas be rollin' deep," Bills said.

"So what should we do?" Reign asked.

"I know where Bigz stays at. I say we go through and get him." Chino stated.

"Wait, wait, wait," Power said.

They all looked at Power.

"You really wanna go at them East Side niggas?" Power asked, testing Chino.

"Hell yea,"

"Why would you wanna help us so much if my dad is gone and your connect's gone? What you tryna pull Chino?"

Power looked into Chino's eyes.

Chino sighed. "Okay, okay you got me. Maybe I don't wanna go at these Eastside cats *just* because y'all my lil' niggas."

"What the fuck you planning' then?" Reign asked mad.

"It's simple. We take out the Eastside fools then we take all their business."

"But you lost your connect. What's the point of takin' business if you got no dope?" Bills asked.

"Y'all niggas can be my new connect."

"How?" Reign asked.

Loyalty Is Blind

"Waters is gone. I'm sure you know yo papi's connect Power. You can get him to put you on, and I'll buy it all off you up front. That way, I can get it a lot cheaper and hit off my connect who aint got shit. Then y'all can drop the prices and compete wit' Sammy Smooth. You can probably even get it lower than Sammy Smooth."

Chino's plan did sound like a very good idea.

"Yea. We can take Waters' spot," Bills said.

"We can divide all the business we got now, plus the Eastside's business, and even Waters business that he had."

"He's right. This does sound good," Reign admitted.

"I gotta see if my pop's connect will even do business wit me," Power said.

"If he's a real businessman, he will." Chino said.

"Well what we waitin for? Let's get these Eastside niggas." Reign said.

Chino went and scooped up Smoke. They all drove up to the spot where Bigz was. It was a tall building, an apartment complex. They were all dressed in black Champion hoodies and sweat pants with ski masks folded up on top of their heads. They were ready for anything.

"Is this the spot right here?" Bills asked.

"Si, we gotta do this shit quick. Remember, it's an apartment complex so that means we gotta be quiet , or mutha fucka's gonna be nosey and call the popo," Chino said.

"Aight, so we just gon knock his ass out and bring him in the car," Bills said.

"What if he got mad niggas in there?" Reign asked.

"Then we get loud. Ya know dat" Smoke said, cocking his gun.

Loyalty Is Blind

"That's right, and then we split up and meet at the checkpoint. If we get out quick, the cops aint gonna chase us. They gonna be happy that there's dead brothas and Latinos," Chino said.

"A'ight. Nobody get in my way and just watch how *Buckshot Bills* does this," Bills said.

Power sucked his teeth.

"Bills, shut yo' dumb ass up," Reign said.

"Nigga don't talk to me like that while I'm in mission mode. You never know what could happen. I don't even know what could happen. I coulda just snapped right there." Bills said.

Reign punched Bills in his arm.

"Ouch!" Bills yelled in pain.

"Stop fuckin' around nigga. I a'int got time for your bullshit," Reign said.

"A'ight, you got that. You can hit me when we cramped up in a car, but if we was in an open field, I would fuck you up."

Reign ignored Bills and pulled down his ski mask. "Cmon niggas. We wastin time."

***

They walked into the apartment building and tried to walk up the stairs as quiet as they could. The passed a bunch of apartments in the hallway. Luckily no one was up that late and left out of their apartments or they would have been spotted, they walked up to Bigz' door. They all stood outside the door to the apartment that Bigz was in. They could hear the radio blasting loud. Good for them because it would drown out noise.

Loyalty Is Blind

Smoke pulled out a big, thick, sturdy screw driver, and quietly slid it under the door. He lifted it a bit so they could see inside the apartment. Bills crouched down and looked under. No one was near the door. Chino pulled out his lock picking supplies, and quickly unlocked the door. Chino would never get rusty. His break in skills were still sharp. The lock clicked and Reign slowly pushed the door open. Power walked into the apartment behind his .9mm, followed by everyone else. Chino quietly shut the door behind himself.

They could hear people in the living room down the hall as the radio bumped. Chino carefully peeked his head around the corner and spotted four men smoking weed and counting money. One of them was Bigz. Chino looked back at The Cipher and Smoke. He put up a thumbs up, and then put up for fingers. They got what he was saying. They rushed in the room. Bigz and his people had no idea what was happening. The Cipher, Chino, and Smoke had Bigz and his boys on the ground at gunpoint in seconds.

"Take whatever you want!" Bigz yelled.

"Shut your bitch ass up!" Reign yelled, just under the volume of the music.

Suddenly one of the back room doors opened up and a man came out shooting. A bullet hit Smoke in the shoulder.

"Ugh," Smoke grunted in pain.

They all took their attention off of the men in the ground and all shot at the man who just hit Smoke. The man jerked around as bullets crashed into different parts of his body. The man fell to the ground and died. One of the men on the ground pulled out a gun and pointed it at Chino's back.

Bang!

Bills shot him in the head, saving Chino's life. Chino

Loyalty Is Blind

turned around in shock. He quickly gave Bills a thankful look.

Bigz passed everyone and ran in a room, and his two men followed. They all started to shoot at them. Power hit one in the back. Chino caught one in the leg and he stumbled to the ground. Reign stepped on his back and shot the back of his head. Bigz made it in the room, grabbed a pump shotgun and he loaded it. They all could hear the loud, threatening load of the gun.

Oh shit! Chino thought.

Then Bigz jumped out of the room, into the hallway, and started shooting at all of them. They all ducked for cover as the pump shotgun's bullets chopped up the TV, sofa, lamps, and walls. Bigz cocked the shotgun several times. Red shells jumped out of the side of the gun and hit the ground and he let shots go.

"That's a nice fuckin gun," Bills said.

"You a'ight Smoke!?" Chino yelled over the gunfire.

"Yea bruh, I'll be good Ya' know dat!" Smoke yelled, breathing heavy.

Power pointed his gun around the corner, with his body still in cover. He let off shots in a blind fire. Power heard the gunfire stop as Bigz grunted and fell to the floor. Power ran around the corner and dashed straight at Bigz. Bigz went to point his gun at Power, but he quickly pushed it to the side and butted Bigz with his gun. Bigz dropped the pump shotgun and started to cry for his life.

"Please yo, take what you want. Just let me live. I got mad money under my mattress in the back room. I just got mad bread recently, you can have it all just-"

Bang!

Loyalty Is Blind

Power shot Bigz in his dick. Bigz let out a piercing squeal.

"Ahhh-Urrgh," His scream was cut short when his mouth got filled up with the barrel of Power's gun.

Bigz' eyes opened wide, in terror. He couldn't scream, only hum loud. Power pulled the trigger. Pieces of the back of Bigz' head painted the wall behind him. His body slumped to the side as blood bubbled out of his mouth and soaked his dead body and clothes. They all heard police sirens, and knew the police were right outside.

"Fuck!" Reign yelled.

Reign and Chino ran into the back room and flipped the mattress over. They found where Bigz put Waters' money. There was more money than any of them ever seen. They ripped the sheet off the mattress, quickly tossed all of the money into it, and rapped it up like a sack. The cops started to come in the building. They all ran out of Bigz' apartment. Reign was holding the sheet full of money. They could hear the police running up the stairs. Bills opened up a random apartment door.

"C'mon!" Bills yelled.

They all ran into the random apartment. That's all they could do.

Loyalty Is Blind

Chapter 15

They entered the apartment and saw a girl lying on a coach, in a living room, which was completely dark. It was only lit by a dim TV flashing different colors around the room. She looked to be about seventeen. She looked over at them, and her eyes widened in fear. Bills ran up and pointed his gun at her before the fear in her eyes made it out her mouth.
"Don't make a noise or I gotta kill you," Bills whispered. The girl nodded, in fear.
"Who else in the crib wit' you?" Bills asked.
"Just my gramma."
"Bills pointed down the hall. Reign went toward where Bills pointed, and walked into a room at the end of the hall. Reign saw a little old lady sleeping on her back with tubes running out of her nose. There was an oxygen tank next to her bed. She looked like she could die any second. He walked up to the old lady and she didn't flinch. She barely looked alive. He tapped her stomach with the gun. She still didn't move. Reign raised an eye. "Hey. Wake up."
Still nothing. He looked around and then gently pushed her stomach. There was still no movement. Reign put his ear to her mouth, and he heard her soft breaths. She was alive.
"Yo!" Reign yelled.
The old lady remained in her slumber. Reign scratched his head.
Chino checked the sheet full of money that they brought back. He opened it and discovered about 100 stacks. He smiled and closed it back up.
Power peeked out the peephole, and could see the police

Loyalty Is Blind

running down the hallway.

"Don't worry. We just gonna chill here fo a little while. We'll be up outta here soon. Just keep watchin' TV," Bills instructed her as he nudged his head toward the TV.

He looked at the TV and seen the girl was watchin' *Dragon Ball*.

"Girl, you in here watchin' Dragon Ball?" Bills said, amazed.

The girl had no idea what to say. She was confused at what was going on. One second she was watching cartoons. The next second she's got 5 niggas in masks around her apartment.

"This is my favorite show," Bills said, excited as he sat down next down next to the girl.

Smoke sat in a corner. He was in pain with a hot bullet lodged in his shoulder.

"You gon be a'ight?" Chino asked, concerned.

"Yea, we gotta go outta town and go to the hospital tomorrow my nigga," Smoke said.

"You can hang a whole day?"

"Yea, I got this. I just need rest. Ya know dat bruh."

Smoke's face was pale. He fell asleep and laid in the corner.

"So what's your name?" Bills asked the girl.

She was uncomfortable and scared but she thought it was a good idea to make some type of talk with Bills, she answered.

"Lisa," her voice was shaky.

"Don't worry Lisa. We just waitin for them cops to bounce, and then we gonna leave. You like Dragon Ball?"

"Yea."

Loyalty Is Blind

Bills liked that. She was a 17 year old girl who liked Dragon Ball. That right there said a little about her. It said that she had her own mind and didn't follow people to fit in. Power still looked out the peep hole. He could see the cops walking back and forth investigating shit. Reign walked back in the living room, and said.

"Is yo' gramma okay?"

"She's fine. She just real old," Lisa said.

"Aight," Reign said with a shrug.

There was a loud knock at the door.

"It's the boys," Power whispered in a panic.

They all started to pace around. Bills held his head with both hands, Smoke still slept, and Chino ran and hid behind a curtain.

"What the fuck the police want?" Bills asked.

"They just investigatin shit. They probably wanna ask questions," Power said.

Lisa had no idea what to do. She looked around at everyone running around. Bills even juked a couple times then did a spin. Reign pulled out his .45 and pointed it right in Lisa's face.

"Look here bitch. You gonna answer that door and tell them pigs that everything's fine. You aint heard or seen shit. You say or do *anything* sketchy, we all gonna be some dead mutha' fuckas in here." Reign's voice was fierce and serious.

Lisa nodded in agreement and fear.

A detective leaned on the wall of Lisa's doorway. He looked down the hallway, watching his fellow officers talk to other people in their apartments. Then he banged on the door louder.

"Police! Open up!" he yelled.

Loyalty Is Blind

A sleepy eyed teenage girl opened the door.
She looked at the cop.
"Is there a problem officer?" her voice was groggy.
"Sorry for waking you. I just need to ask you a few questions. This will only take a minute."
Lisa yawned, "Okay."
"Are your parent's home?"
"No, I don't got parents. I live here with my gramma. She's very tired though. She aint bout to wake up for nothin."
"Alright, but did you hear any shooting from the apartments a few doors down?"
"No, I was just tryin to sleep. Those guys play loud music all the time. I usually always hear them making noise all night so I try to ignore them."
"Did you see anything suspicious today?"
"No, it's been a normal day. What happened?"
"A couple people were murdered a couple doors down from your apartment. I'm just making sure you're fine."
Murdered? Lisa thought.
She was pretty much being held hostage by these murderers. She had to cooperate and find a way out of this.
"Thanks for your concern. I'm fine though."
"Goodnight ma'am."
"Goodnight officer," Lisa said as she closed the door.
She looked at Reign who was holding the gun to her face.
"Good job," he said.
Hours passed. Forensics investigated shit and the cops were investigating shit. Everyone except for Reign fell asleep. Bills sat up, asleep on the couch, next to Lisa, who had herself rolled up in a ball with her shirt covering her whole body. The police started to pack up and were leaving.

Loyalty Is Blind

Reign woke everyone up. "The police is bouncin'. We gotta get up outta here without getting caught."

Chino carefully moved the shade on the window to peek outside. He saw all of the police packing up and leaving.

"We gotta get outta here. Smoke needs treatment," Chino said.

Reign nodded, and then asked. "Well what should we do with this chick and her gramma?"

Lisa could hear them talking. She only acted like she was asleep so she could eavesdrop.

"I don't know. Maybe we should shoot her to make sure she don't talk," Chino said.

Lisa got scared. She thought of running and screaming. She didn't want to get shot.

"Shut y'all dumb asses up. We aint shootin nobody. She helped us," Bills said.

"We gotta think about ourselves nigga. What if she tells on us? You can't be saving people and shit. Stop actin' soft," Reign said.

"I don' give a fuck what you say. We aint shootin her. We don' hit women or kids, that's the rule. You always tryna shoot somebody." Bills said

"It was only an idea niggas. I didn't mean to start nothing," Chino said, putting his hands up.

"I don't give a fuck bout no damn *rules*. I'll shoot anything, whether it's a nigga, a bitch, a gramma, an uncle, a dog, a cat, or a fish. I'll shoot a damn tree. I don't give a fuck nigga," Reign said.

"Well fuck you and your tree shootin' ass. We aint shootin' her." Bils said.

"Everybody chill. We a'int gonna shoot her. The gun

Loyalty Is Blind

would make too much noise and we would hafta run. We gotta get out of here nice and quiet with stealth," Power said. Everyone looked at each other, and nodded in agreement.

"Somebody wake up Smoke. We gotta get up outta here," Reign said.

The Cipher, Smoke, and Chino made a successful escape. They split up and went to their houses. Bills took sheet full of money to his house because Power didn't want to bring it around Sylph. Reign was worried that his parents could find it and steal it for crack and Chino had to drive to the next city over to bring smoke to the hospital. He didn't want to drive with anything in the car.

***

Power went to Sylph's house. He crept around to her window quietly because he didn't want to wake her on the couch. It was 4:30 in the morning and he wanted to sleep. He didn't feel like listening to all of her questions because he *definitely* didn't want to answer them. He carefully pressed his hands on the window to push it up. It barely moved an inch. Power froze because he had to be quieter. The window suddenly flew wide open it slammed up at the top making a loud noise. Power fell backward onto his ass. Sylph poked her head out the window quickly. She looked at the man that she stayed awake for all night.

Power! What the fuck took you so long? I been waitin all night."

Sylph definitely took Reign's advice. She was being a lot tougher, and Power liked it. He would never admit it though.

"Sylph. What the fuck's wrong with you? Be quiet, you gonna wake someone up."

Loyalty Is Blind

"Hurry up and get inside."

Power climbed in the window. Sylph hugged him. He really didn't like how Sylph was acting like she was his girlfriend. Well, he actually did like it but he didn't want to bring Sylph in his shit with him. Sylph deserved better than the life Power lead. He decided it was time to keep it real and tell Sylph the truth.

"Love, I know you like me, and you know I like you but, it just aint gonna work right now. I don't wanna fuck your life up. You deserve way better than me. It's hard to explain. I really like you but it aint gonna work right now. I'm just not ready yet."

I'm just not ready yet.

That was damn near all Sylph heard Power say. *Not ready yet. As in, will be ready later.*

She thought to herself.

Just take it slow. You got forever to be with him.

Sylph could wait. She smiled and kissed Power on the cheek.

"My bad Power. I just was real worried. I'm happy to see you're alright. Let's get some rest."

Power and Sylph slept in the same bed, but Power slept with his back to her. Sylph ached for Power to hold her, but she held her composure. Power also wanted to turn around and hold Sylph, but he didn't, to protect her from himself. So they both ached for each other and went to sleep.

Loyalty Is Blind

Chapter 16

Bills went shopping at the mall. He was leaving until he noticed Lisa also leaving, about to start walking to her apartments. He walked up to her.

"Excuse me. May I walk you home?" He asked Lisa with a half-smile on his face.

Lisa looked at Bills. "I don't talk to strangers."

Her tone was playful.

"Me, a stranger?! You know me! *Dolla, dolla, Bills y'all!*" Bills said, spreading his arms and nodding his head.

Lisa knew Bills' name. He was a pretty well-known person around the city.

Lisa giggled at Bills, "You don't even know me."

"What you talkin' about? I know you. I always had a crush on you, but I was too shy to tell you," Bills lied.

"Haha, yea, okay. You being shy? Sure, you don't even like me."

"For real, I think about you all the time. I aint scared to say it no more, so I wanna walk you home and talk about it."

Lisa laughed at Bills jokes, but she wanted to play hard to get.

"Buh bye Bills," Lisa chimed as she walked off, hoping Bills would follow.

Bills jogged up next to her and sang *All the Time* by Troop.

"I can't wait to get to school each day, and wait for you to pass my way, and bells start to ring and angels start to sing."

Lisa chuckled as Bills sang louder.

Loyalty Is Blind

"Hey that's the girl for you, so what are you gonna do." Lisa walked, holding shopping bags as Bills followed, dancing around and signing in his voice that he swore was great.

"All I do is think of you day and night. I can't get you out my mind."

The other people shopping in the mall started to look at the scene Bills was making. Lisa started to feel embarrassed.

"Bills. Everyone's looking at us. They gonna think-"

"*All the timmee!*" Bills sang as loud as he could, while holding his arm up and posing like he was in the Five Heartbeats.

"C'mon Bills, you can walk me home," Lisa said, just wanting to get away from this awkward situation.

Bills walked Lisa home. Lisa loved how he held himself like a respectful gentle-man. He was very funny. and could talk about anything. They got to her apartment.

"Okay Bills. This is my spot. Thanks for walkin' me home."

"No problem. I got you anytime."

Lisa looked deep into Bills' dark eyes. He could tell she wanted to kiss him. She leaned in near his face. Bills slid right past her and walked straight into her apartment. He walked to the couch and lounged across it.

"What are you doin' Bills? What if my dad was here or something?"

Bills knew she only lived with her grandmother. So he calmly picked up the remote, flipped through channels and said.

"I'm not worried about yo' daddy. I'm a cool mutha' fucka and everybody likes me. Besides, I'm undefeated, I

116

Loyalty Is Blind

can't lose a fight."

Lisa liked Bills' confidence.

"I really don't even live with my daddy anyways."

"Word? Well now you just gotta worry about your moms fallin' in love wit' me."

"Aint nobody fallin' in love wit' you Bills. And I don't live wit' my momma either. I live wit' my gramma. It's just the two of us here."

"For real?" Bills played dumb.

"Yea, and I gotta help her out today. I'm gonna be real busy, so you gotta go."

She really didn't want him to leave, but she didn't want him to sit around bored all day. If he thought she was boring, then he might not like her.

"You really want me to leave?" Bills said, while showing a playful puppy face.

Lisa looked at Bills. She knew he wasn't really sad, but it still got her. Bills' charm was amazing. She actually felt bad.

"No, I didn't say I want you to leave." Lisa said, in a tone like she just accidentally stepped on a puppy.

"A'ight, then I'ma chill out for a little while," Bills said, plainly.

"But you gunna be bored."

"No I aint, trust me, *Bojack Bills* don't get bored."

"Bojack Bills?"

"That's right."

Lisa wasn't even gonna ask who or what that was. She had to cook for her grandmother. She took some pots and pans down and got everything ready. She heated up some grease and put some chicken in flour.

"You cook?" Bills asked.

Loyalty Is Blind

"Yea, what you thought this was?"

"Oh yea? Well this is what we gonna do. You gonna cook me some fried chicken, you gonna make me some cherry Kool Aid wit' extra sugar, shaken not stirred, and you gonna make me some good rice wit' that and bring it all to me on this couch."

Lisa rose an eye at Bills.

"What you think I'm your maid?"

"Listen, if you wanna be my girl, you *gotsta* have skills. Cookin's just one thing you better be good at," Bills said, in a joking but confident tone.

"And who said I wanna be your girl?"

"Lisa, stop playin' games and cook me something," Bills said, with his half smile then wink.

Lisa rolled her eyes as she smiled at Bills. She cooked for her grandmother and Bills. He devoured the food and sat and watched TV. It was getting late.

"Bills, you been here all day, it's getting' late."

"So what? I never sleep, cuz sleep is the cousin of death."

"What the hell are you talkin about?"

Bills stretched out and lay down on the couch. He kicked his shoes off, and put his feet on Lisa's legs.

"You wouldn't understand. It's a genius thing," Bills said as he yawned and closed his eyes.

"I thought you never sleep."

"I'm not sleepin', I'm restin' my eyes."

"You can't sleep here."

Lisa was ashamed that she didn't have a bed to sleep on.

"Lisa, go to sleep," Bills said as he tried to sleep.

Lisa curled up and lay next to him. Bills opened his eyes and looked into Lisa's eyes. She leaned in to kiss him.

Loyalty Is Blind

"Hold up," Bills said, interrupting her kiss.

"What's wrong?"

"You know how far a kiss could go. I got plans on keepin you around for a little while. You got time for all that later." Lisa smiled as she looked at Bills. She liked everything about him. He was so confident, outgoing, funny, nice and smooth. He already had her. Lisa fell asleep on Bills' chest.

***

The next day Chino brought Smoke to the hospital. Bills and Reign met up to count out the money wrapped up in the sheet. They put it all in a duffle bag that Reign had at his house. Power went to Wasala's. This day a lot of shit would change. Chino made a plan with Power to cop dope off of him from Wasala. The Cipher would make more money than ever before. They would start their conquest to take over the city. They were stronger and smarted than ever and with Chino on their side, they were an obvious force. Chino had control over a vast number of 730s foot soldiers and generals. They were growing with every dollar that was made. Whatever the Cipher would say, Chino would agree with, which basically put them in control of the 730s, thanks to Chino's loyal and humble mindset.

***

"Wasala. I need your help. My father passed and I plan on taking over his business," Power said.

Wasala looked into Power's eyes. He didn't want Power to live that life, but Power might resent him if he denied his help, which was so easy to grant.

Loyalty Is Blind

"Power, are you sure about this? I will help you, but I feel that you can do so much more than this," Wasala said.

"Yes Wasala, I'm sure. Thought about it all. I still plan on finishing school and going to college. I plan on really doing something with my life. This right here would greatly advance me. I really need your help. I don't got a father no more, your all I got Wasala. Please don't let me down."

Wasala's heart warmed because he loved Power. He was a young man who was so special and smart, submitted to Allah, and always stayed humble, while trying to obtain what men have never obtained in a lifetime. Power stood before Wasala, not even noticing his own accomplishments. Just by attempting to buy from Wasala was an amazing feat. Wasala took it as an honor that Power would look up to him like a father. Of course he would help Power. He would do anything Power ever asked for.

"Power. I will be honest with you. I do not desire for you to attempt this form of life. That being said, I will do anything for you. I love you like my own son. I would kill for you, die for you, and everything in between. The answer is yes. I will support you in any way you need. I only ask that you come to me if you need help, and please try to follow the path of Allah. Never ever forget Allah. I am proud of you Power. You deserve every blessing in life."

Power almost couldn't believe it. The words echoed in his mind.

I am proud of you Power.

The words he searched for from his father for 15 years, he now got from a man who surpassed Waters in every way. Power looked deep into Wasala's eyes, he nodded his head.

"Thank you father."

Loyalty Is Blind

Wasala gave Power a warming, honored smile and put his hand on Power's shoulder.

"You will always be welcome my son."

Loyalty Is Blind

Loyalty Is Blind

Chapter 17

Power went back to Chino's spot, with really good news and a bag full of really good dope. They would all be so excited. Wasala even decided to give it to Power for lower then Waters used to get it for, making it so they could compete with Sammy Smooth. Power walked in the room with a big smile on his face, and dropped the bag of dope on the ground. Everyone jumped up in excitement as they all chanted and laughed. They all dapped Power, and Chino put Power in a playful headlock. Chino pushed Power back and pulled out two thick wads of cash, held together by thick rubber bands. He could barely fit the fat stacks in his hands.

"I'll buy most of this shit right now," Chino said.

Chino bought most of it right off Power on the spot. Right there Power already made more than Wasala wanted back, and he still had some dope left. He made so much profit off Chino that he just threw the rest to Reign and Bills.

"We still got this shit to split too," Smoke said, lifting up the duffle bag, full of the money they got from Bigz

They opened up the duffle bag and poured stack after stack onto the carpet. Reign and Bills already counted it out previously and separated it in five stacks of around $20,000. They quickly split. It was a little more than what Power just made off of Chino, and nothing to what Bills and Reign were about to make off the free dope they just got. The Cipher, Smoke, and Chino huddled up.

"From now on, y'all lil niggas run the city. I just run wit y'all. I owe everythin to y'all." Chino said.

Power smiled, then said. "Good lookin' out Chino. We couldn't have done nothin without you."

Loyalty Is Blind

"Y'all lil' niggas is the strongest team I ever seen. I had to get down wit' you niggas right when I peeped y'all." Chino told them.

"You right Chino, but you know we got mad love for you." Power replied.

"The Cipher's on top baby!" Bills shouted.

Chino smiled and put his fist out. "730 Cipher!"

Everyone put their fist in the middle, and touched fists at the same time they yelled.

The Cipher came up more than they ever have in their lives. Over the years, Reign and Bills eventually took over all of the business that Chino didn't have. Reign dropped the price lower then Sammy Smooth's, and eventually ended up supplying Sammy Smooth himself. Power still had Waters' old black book, and gave it to Bills. He made it Bills who took over Waters' old business. Chino made more money than ever by getting the dope from Power for a lot lower than his old connect. Power just sat back and supplied his boys. The operation was flawless. No one had anything to complain about. The guys from the Eastside still had a moderately large group, and they knew that The Cipher killed Bigz. They plotted, but the Cipher wasn't worried because they could send their army of 730s on any trouble.

Reign moved out, and left his crack head parents. He grew up to own many corner stores and a jewelry shop. Bills moved his family to a bigger home, his family's struggles were no more. He moved his mother and his brother Maleek, who was now 10, to a new house. He built a relationship with Lisa, and she moved in with him.

In 2010, Bills and Lisa had a healthy baby boy, name William Benjamin. He chased his dream and became an

Loyalty Is Blind

expert martial artist in Kung Fu and Wu Shu. He eventually ended up owning many dojo's across the city and even was a teacher at some of the classes in his favorite dojo, *The Kage Dojo*. One of his new nicknames was Bills sensei. Smoke stacked up and bought a couple stores. He owned a Southern Soul-Food restaurant called *Smokey's*. He used it to clean his money.

Power lived by himself, in his own house nicknamed *Power Palace*. He invested a lot in stocks and real estate, after he dropped out of college, and his business couldn't be doing better. The Cipher paid for Sylph to live in her own house. Every time The Cipher or Chino or Smoke stepped foot in Academy Homes Projects they were treated like kings. Everyone respected them, they had it all.

Hasad left Wasala's at age twenty three and grew to be one of the most feared professional underground assassins. He still would visit Wasala, but The Cipher hasn't seen much of him. They knew his presence when they would see or hear about a dead judge, politician, or mayor. He killed in many ways. Old fashion murder, armed or unarmed, poisoned food, sabotaged vehicles. Sometimes the people would straight up disappear. Hasad had countless bodies, and no one would dare go against him. The Cipher has never crossed paths with him in a negative way. Reign respected Hasad deeply, but always thought about killing him to prove dominant supremacy. Hasad felt the same way about Reign, but they both had pure respect for each other, so they never clashed.

Power and Sylph's relationship was still fucked up. As Power grew in his business more incidents happened, and more situations popped up. He felt he wanted her further and further away. Sylph still stayed loyal to an unmoved Power, and never once tried to move on. They both shared a solid mutual love for each other, but Power wanted better for Sylph. She always felt that Power was all she ever wanted. She didn't care about the lifestyle or anything else. She loved Power, and that was that.

Loyalty Is Blind

Chapter 15
June 2016

Power was in the office of his mansion, sitting on his office chair. A mountain of cash sat on the desk in front of him, next to a $20,000 portable money counter, a mini Uzi, a bottle of Louie the 13th, an M9, 3 cell phones, and an iPad that had an app that controlled almost everything in his whole mansion. Power took a swig of the Louie as he placed a wad of money in the money counter. He grabbed his iPad and pointed it at the stereo, and then turned it on. The song *Stack It Up* by Gambit, blasted out the speakers.

The song played as the alcohol soothed his body.

You gotta pick it up add it up, break it down bag it up, grind it out stack it up, do it all again.

You gotta pick it up add it up, break it down bag it up, grind it out stack it up, homie you gon' win.

The money counter made a quiet hum, as the hundred dollar bills flipped and stacked on each other neatly as the numbers counted up in the 6 figure digits. Power nodded his head to the music.

I stacks 'em up like cement bricks tell papi to send em in/
my coke don't even look like sugar I got that cinnamon/
I'm sick wit it when it comes to flippin' shit/
this shit is simple kid these fiends aint tryna be shiverin'/
this the best shit around you can't tell me nothing'/
that's why niggas eyes water when they smell these onions.

Power looked on one of his security monitors and saw a BMW X7 parked up the street, and then his cell phone rang.

He looked at his iPhone and saw it was Sylph calling. He answered.

"What's good Love?"

"Nothin', just kinda depressed at the moment. I'm parked outside sippin' on this Remy."

"Well come over, and save me some of that bottle."

"It's all gone, I drank it already,"

Power sucked his teeth. "Whateva, just come through."

He hung up and watched Sylph drive her X7 up to his house on his monitor. She got out of her car and walked up to the front door.

He grabbed the iPad, and pressed his thumb on the screen. The iPhone beeped indicating that it was now unlocked to do whatever Power wanted it to do. It could now do a lot more than turn on lights, radios, and TV's. Power pressed the button to unlock the front door. When he saw Sylph walk in and close the door behind herself, he locked the door again. He looked at his desk with blood money and guns on it. He didn't want Sylph seeing any of this shit. He slid all of the cash on the table into a big sturdy Gucci duffle bag. He put the mini Uzi in a drawer of his desk, and put the portable money counter in another drawer. He picked up the iPad and pointed it at an empty wall, and then punched a code in. A piece of the wall slid open, revealing a secret compartment. He picked up the big Gucci bag full of money, and put it in the secret compartment. He went back to his sofa, sat down and pointed the iPad at the secret compartment, closed it, and made it look like a normal empty wall again. He pointed the iPad to the dead fire place, pressed on the screen, and the fire place sprang to life. The flames danced around the glass prism. He pointed the iPad at the 60'

Loyalty Is Blind

LG TV and turned it on.

Sylph walked into the room as Power lounged on his sofa. He could tell she was drunk. He looked at Sylph and thought. *Damn, you're so beautiful.* In a cool tone his mouth said something totally different.

"Sup Love? You look a'ight today."

"Thanks."

Power tore his eyes off Sylph, and placed them on the TV, which wasn't even making noise because the volume was down and some documentary was on. The music still blasted. Sylph strutted toward Power and picked up the Louie the 13th. When she moved the bottle, Power saw he left an M9 on the table. Power let out a frustrated sign, walked to the desk, grabbed the gun, and concealed it on his waist. Sylph rolled her eyes as she took a sip of Louie.

Like I never saw a gun before. Why is he always acting so scary? Sylph thought to herself.

Sylph put down the bottle and went to give Power a kiss. Power moved his head back and avoided the kiss.

"C'mon Love. Chill wit' all that. You drunk right now."

Sylph couldn't stand Power's unbreakable will.

"Why the fuck you always playin' that shit wit me? You know you love me."

"Love, I aint in the mood for this shit. You already know what it is. I don't want you around all this shit."

"I know you don't baby, but I'm part of this team. So just accept it."

"I aint acceptin' shit. I want better shit for you. I can give you enough paper to get you in Harvard, and get your own shit so you can have a real life, wit' no risks."

"I don't want none of that fancy shit. All I want is you."

Loyalty Is Blind

Power hated these mushy conversations. It made him feel soft and uncomfortable. He snatched the Louie and downed another shot.

"C'mon Love, I don't wanna talk about this shit."

"Why can't you just be real wit me? Keep it fuckin real Power."

"I am keepin' it real."

"Oh really? Well then, do you love me?"

"What?" Power sked, trying to stall the inevitable.

"Do. You. Love. Me?" each word was clear as air.

Power let out an uncomfortable sigh as he rubbed his head.

"Yea Sylph. I fucking love you like a sister."

Sylph rolled her eyes at her lying love. She couldn't stand it when he lied. She leaned in close to him.

"Power, are you *in* love wit' me?"

Power's heart skipped a beat. His mind said the truth, his mouth lied.

Yes, his heart said.

"No," Power told her.

She looked into his eyes. Even though she knew he was lying, it still hurt bad for him to say that. Her eyes began to fill with tears. He hated to see her hurt. He let out a sigh.

"Love, don cry. It's just that-"

Smack!

Sylph cocked back and smacked the shit out of Power. He looked back at her with fury in his eyes. He grabbed her by both arms.

"Are you fuckin stupid!? Don't *ever* put your fuckin hands on me!" Power yelled as he shook her.

She flailed around, trying to hit Power.

Loyalty Is Blind

"Fuck you Power! What did I do wrong for you to treat me like this? I would do *anything* for you! All you do is run away from me!"

"Shut up Sylph! I'm tired of your bullshit!"

"I been holdin it down, and waiting for 10 years!"

"Chill your ass out and-"

"10 fucking years! And you gonna sit here in my face and tell me you don't love me!? After all the shit I did for you!" she yelled as loud as she could as tears fell down her cheeks.

"I been told you the deal, but you won't stop pushin' me!"

"What's wrong wit' me? I love you! Why don't you love me? What am I doing wrong?

"Aint nothin wit' you. It's all me!"

"Why don't you love me? Why can't you-"

"I love you!"

The room became dead silent.

Loyalty Is Blind

Chapter 19

Power still held Sylph as he looked into her teary eyes. She calmed down and started to breathe slower. Power sighed and loosened his grip on her arms, and then said in a softer tone.

"I love you Sylph."

It was hard for Power to say it, but he felt Sylph deserved to hear the truth. He was tired of keeping his feelings bottled up.

She took a deep breath. She waited so long to hear those wonderful words. She rested her cheek on Power's chest.

"I love you too Power."

Power hugged Sylph, and held her close. He cherished every second he ever held Sylph, and thanked Allah that he had the opportunity to experience the presence of Sylph and all the bliss that came with her. He inhaled he sweet sent.

"It's just, I love you so much that I don't want you in no shit. You can do so much better than all this shit. You can do so much better than *me*."

"You're all I ever wanted. I don't care what you think. Aint nothin in my life better then you. If I wanted anything else, I wouldn't have waited for you for this long."

"I know. I know. It's all fucked up."

"Baby, I drank a little too much. I need to lie down. Let's go to your room and watch a movie."

Power sighed and then took a deep breath. He knew Sylph was only trying to get in his bed.

"Love, stop playin games, 'cause you aint getting in my bed."

"I promise I won't try nothin slick. I really need to lie

Loyalty Is Blind

down and rest, I swear." Sylph said, as she looked into Power's eyes, with a sad and innocent look on her face.

Power took a long deep breath as he looked at Sylph's beautiful, but sad face. He promised himself that he wouldn't let her go too far.

"A'ight, let's go," Power said, picking up Sylph and bringing her to his room.

This was Power's master bedroom, on his wall he had a 104 inch custom HD movie projector. Sylph loved watching movies on it. It felt like you was really in the movie. Power gently placed Sylph on his comfy bed on top of the big, fluffy, thick, 10,000 thread count Egyptian cotton covers.

"I'ma go grab a new bottle since your drunk ass wanna drink everything up," Power said.

"Shut up nigga. Put in a movie," Sylph slurred jokingly.

Power laughed at Sylph as he walked to the projector and put the Blu Ray disk in. The projector beamed out images, and the whole wall turned into a movie. He walked downstairs, to the bar, an grabbed a bottle of Hennessy Paradis. He took a sip and the liquor went down like cool water. From drinking the Hennessy Paradis and the Louie earlier, Power was fucked up. He grabbed the bottle and a half smoked blunt out of the ashtray. Then he walked to the small refrigerator, and grabbed a gallon of cool orange juice then poured it into a glass then he grabbed a bag of Jolly Ranchers off the top of the fridge and walked back to his room. When he walked in Sylph was under the covers, watching the movie.

"Come cuddle with me."

"Girl, chill your ass out. You letting that Remy talk for you."

Loyalty Is Blind

"Be quiet and get in bed."

Power walked to his nightstand next to his bed, and placed the Henny, Jolly Ranchers, and glass of orange juice down. He took his spring loaded knife out of his pocket and placed it on the nightstand. Then took his M9 off of his waist and placed it next to his knife. He kicked off his white Top Tens and slid off his jeans he had on Adidas basketball shorts and Adidas socks. He took off his fresh white t-shirt and had on a tank top. He took a lighter out of the drawer in the night stand and lit the blunt in his mouth. He took a drag, grabbed the Henny, popped the cap, and took a swig and sat on the bed next to Sylph.

"Gimmie some of that orange juice."

"*Gimmie* got his neck broke."

Sylph rolled her eyes and sighed. Power laughed as he handed her the glass of orange juice, and then he popped a Jolly Rancher in his mouth.

"Let me get one. Green Apple's my favorite."

Power shrugged as he pointed to his mouth.

"A'int no more green apple. I'm eatin' the last one."

Sylph grabbed his head and started kissing him. When she stopped, she had the Jolly Rancher in her mouth, she stuck her tongue out at him showing him the candy in her mouth. Power hit the blunt as he looked at her like she was crazy.

"You can't be kissin' me. One thing leads to another, another thing leads to your back being broke," Power joked. The liquor was starting to hit him hard. He shook his head and got serious.

"Nah, but for real. I want you wit' a good man. I don't want you wit' me."

Loyalty Is Blind

She rolled her eyes, she didn't feel like hearing this bullshit.

"Pass me the blunt." She requested.

He passed her the blunt. She took a hit, and then blew out the smoke.

"You know I want you Power. I loved you since we were younger."

He didn't feel like getting into it with her again. It was a calm moment so he just stayed quiet, ignored her, and lay back in his bed. Sylph took another deep pull of the blunt, she held the smoke in her lungs. Then she turned the blunt around and carefully placed the other side of the blunt in her mouth, putting her lips in the middle of the blunt. She grabbed Power's head and blew a shotgun through the blunt, blowing smoke in Power's mouth. He inhaled it, and pressed his lips down on the blunt, then gently slid the blunt out of her mouth, then hit it one good more time, then he grabbed the blunt from his mouth, and put it out on the bag of Jolly Ranchers. Sylph was still in front of his face. She looked deep into Power's green eyes. He started to feel like taking her to his room was a bad idea.

Sylph moved in closer to his face and said.

"I love you Power."

His heart dropped. He had to tell her the truth, he was locked in her beautiful, hazel eyes.

"I love you too Sylph."

Sylph felt relieved of any stress she had. Power was trying to stay strong, and not kiss her, but his will power was fading away. Everything about Sylph was luring him in. Her lips didn't say one word, but they were still calling him to her.

Loyalty Is Blind

They drew closer to each other. She kissed Power with her soft juicy lips. His body gave into her love. He pulled her in close. His will couldn't fight his mind, body, and heart any longer. Power had both hands on Sylph's waist. He trailed his left hand up her body, rubbed up to her face and gently ran his fingers through her smooth silky hair. Their hearts felt like they were on fire. They loved every moment of it. Years and years of holding back was all being let out at that moment. They waited so long for this one moment to happen. Each touch was electrifying, each move was graceful.

Sylph slid her hand under Power's wife beater and started to softly scratch on his stomach, and then she moved her hand down to his basketball shorts. She slid her hand inside, and gently rubbed on him as he got bigger and bigger. She stopped kissing him and looked into his eyes as she still held his dick in her hand. She slowly went down and started sucking the life out of him as she kept eye contact the whole time. He tried to make her stop, but every time he did, it felt even better. It was on. She was sucking his dick like a pro as she kept eye contact.

She didn't even blink once as she looked deep in his eyes as she pleased him. She slowly pulled her face off his dick, her lips smacked when she got off because she was sucking so hard. She licked around the top as she moaned like he was tasty. She licked up and down him and sucked around it.

She kissed his dick with her plump wet lips, and then she put him back inside her mouth and slowly deep throated his whole dick. He couldn't even see his dick anymore, it disappeared inside her face, then she slowly pulled up as she slid both of her hands up and wrapped both of her hands around his shaft. She started bobbing up and down as she slid

Loyalty Is Blind

her hands up and down, and she sucked and bobbed at the top as she made greedy noises.

She wanted to please him so he wouldn't want to go to any other women ever. She promised to make herself perfect in every way. He was about to nut, she stopped and got up. He could see her perfectly clear as the light from the movie flashed different colors on her. They started to undress each other.

They took their time undressing each other. As each thread that was taken off, a worry and insecurity was shed. They slowly unwrapped their precious gifts, and were both pleased at the discovery of each other. Sylph's naked body was perfect, breathtaking, and intricately elaborate. He couldn't see one flaw in her. The sight of Sylph naked made Power want to lick her all over. She stood next to the bed. She stood there with an ass that belonged to an angel. She had a perfect pussy. It looked nice and tight. It was shaved with a little line of hair right above her clit. Her titties sat up perfect like they were fake. She was beautiful. He wanted to nut just from looking at her.

He picked her up, and placed her on the bed. Her body was a great obstacle that he has longed to overcome. They took time traveling around each other's body. Power thanked Allah for every moment. Power was kissing on her lips then he kissed down her neck, down her titties then kissed down to her pussy.

He grabbed both of her ass checks and pulled her in toward him as he filled his face with her pussy. He had her trying to run away from him as she gripped the sheets, softly moaned in pleasure. She was shivering and shaking like she was freezing. She came all over Power's face. Every minute

Loyalty Is Blind

she was having an orgasm. Power stopped eating it and her pussy was dripping wet.

He got up and gently slid his dick inside of her. She moaned in pain when he was entering, but once the strokes went on, she became a monster. She was loving it. The deeper he went, the louder she got.

"Baby, let me ride that dick," she moaned.

Power rolled on his back, Sylph got on top. He held her by her petite waist, and guided her pussy down on his dick. She was tight, her walls were constricted around his joint. She started to ride him to another world. He pushed her waist up and down as he slid in and out of her. Her big titties bounced up and down. She started to scream.

"Daddy I'm about to cum!" she yelled, between moans as her eyes were squinted shut, and she bit her lip.

"Ahh keep goin'. I'm bout to nut too."

They fucked harder and harder until they both came together. Sylph got off of Power and lay next to him. They passed out.

***

A few hours passed. Power held Sylph as they rested naked. She was sound asleep as he watched he breathe. He gently caressed her cheek as he inhaled her sweet sent. He loved every single thing about her. He loved the five senses of her. He loved the sound of her voice, the sight of her beautiful form, the smell of her sent, the touch of her skin, the taste of her lips. He cherished her whole being, he desired her extremely.

Sylph woke up and looked into Power's eyes that watched her sleep. She smiled that beautiful smile. She was

Loyalty Is Blind

so happy that she could finally wake to Power. She waited years and years for this dream to come true. Finally, she got her Power that she yearned for. She wished this moment would last forever. Her love was stronger than ever now. She would do anything in existence for him. She promised herself to never ever lose him.

Power felt so right, but so wrong at the same time. He couldn't believe that he just made love to Sylph. All he could think about was him somehow ruining Sylph's good life. She didn't need to live life with the big risk named Power. He sighed at his own thoughts and how he could ruin a moment as special as this with his own insecurities. Sylph kissed him on the lips. He felt complete the moment their lips touched. He had no more worries, no more doubts, no more insecurity.

He looked into Sylph's beautiful hazel eyes. The moment the kiss was over negative thoughts started to creep from the depths of his mind. He had to somehow tell her that this was a mistake even though he felt it was destiny and even though he didn't want to hide from her love. Deep down he felt like he had to let her go. How does he tell her something like that? He didn't even believe it, but he was forcing himself for the love of her and her living a good life. He loved this moment more than any other, but he loves her too much.

Two months passed. Power and Sylph were hooking up but Power never made it official, he couldn't push himself to have a relationship. Sylph was upset about it, but she still loved him and was happy that he was showing her attention. Power needed to talk to everyone about this situation, he called everyone in for a meeting.

Chapter 17
August 2015

Power called Bills, Reign, and Sylph individually, and told them that he was throwing a team meeting. Bills and Reign showed up early, they didn't have much to do that night. Power wanted to talk to them about Sylph and the way she should be involved in their lives. He felt wrong for letting things get so far with Sylph. He was planning on making it right.

"So what's up? You said we was havin a meetin right?" Sylph asked

"Yea, but you should cook first and we'll talk bout this around the table," Power said.

Sylph gave Power her pretty smile, then strutted toward the kitchen. She made dinner, and they all sat around the table.

"So what's up Power?" Sylph asked, not knowing if she was really ready for this meeting.

"We all gotta talk. Shit still good, but one thing gotta change," Power said.

"A'ight nigga, so what is it?" Bills asked.

"I was thinking and we gotta keep Love out of everythin, she be in too much shit."

Bills sighed, Reign sucked his teeth, Sylph shot Power a glare. They were all getting tired of Power's insecurities when it came to Sylph's safety.

"Are you fucking serious Power?" Sylph spat.

"I don't want you in all this shit." Power stated sharply.

"Fuck you Power. You really need to grow the fuck up

Loyalty Is Blind

and realize that I am a grown ass woman. I'm gonna do whatever the fuck I want."

"Not wit' me you aint. My mom died over this shit, because somebody was trying to get at my pops. I couldn't forgive myself if I ever let that happen to you."

"I gave you everything Power, I gave you *me*! And you just kicked me to the curb like some side hoe."

"Listen, I'm sorry but-"

"First you fuck me, and then you tell me you don't want me, now you tellin' me I can't be part of the team. What the fuck."

"It aint like that Love!"

"Do *not* call me that name. You don't love me."

Those words stung Power. Reign and Bills were really getting sick of Sylph and Power's dramatic soap opera shit. Reign actually liked and appreciated that Sylph always wanted to help them. He felt that she was a grown ass woman and should be able to make her own choices. Bills really didn't care what Sylph's fast ass did, if she wanted to run with the big boys, cool. But no matter what, he always rolled with his boys, right or wrong.

"Power. Love's a grown ass woman. She came up wit' us. I mean, how long you gon be on this shit, she obviously aint gon change her mind." Reign said.

"I don't give a fuck bout any of that shit. I'm saying I don't want her round this shit no more. From now on, shit changing."

Power's mind was made up.

"I feel you Power. I'm down wit' whatever you say," Bills said.

"I'm not a fuckin baby. I'm a twenty-six year old woman.

I helped you a lot, I would do anything for you guys. I aint leaving for nothing."

"Chill yo ass out and-"

"Fuck you! Do you understand how I feel about you? Do you know how you make me feel with all the bullshit you say to me? Do you know what you did to me when you treated me like shit?"

Power didn't know what to say, he sighed as he rubbed his face. Sylph stormed out of the room. Reign sighed and followed her. She raced out of Power's house, to her car.

"Love, wait up!" Reign called out, while jogging up to her.

Sylph ignored him and got in her car. Reign opened the passenger's door and hopped in. Sylph put her head on the steering wheel and cried.

"Why does he do this to me?"

"It's a'ight, he just loves you so much. He don't want you in no shit."

"He doesn't love me. You never do what he did to someone you love."

"I really don't know what to say. Patience leads to benefit. Sometimes people don't know what they got , they never notice the love that was there the whole time."

Sylph wiped away her tears. She thought about what Reign said.

She needed rest, all of this was stressing her out.

"I'm gonna go get some rest."

"A'ight, you be easy Love. I'll be at the crib if you need me."

Sylph let out a frustrated sigh as she wiped away more tears. She leaned over and kissed Reign on the cheek, and said.

"Thanks Reign, goodnight."

Reign nodded, threw up the peace sign and got out the car.

***

Sylph laid in her bed crying, with her face pressed in a tear soaked pillow, as the song "I'm not gon cry" by Mary J Blige played softly on her surround sound.

Well I'm not gon cry, I'm not gon cry, I'm not gon' shed no tears/ No I'm not gon cry, it's not the time, cuz youre not worth my tears.

Who the fuck did Power think he was? How could he fuck her, tell her he wanted nothing to do with her, then tell her she wasn't part of the team. Sylph would do anything for Power, she always loved him but he never showed the same back. Why couldn't he accept that she was a grown ass woman, and was part of the team? Ever since they were kids, Power always tried to keep her out of everything, trying to isolate her from life. She thought back, about the day they killed Bigz.

"Well get some sleep," Reign said, with a nod. *"Because later we gotta meet Chino and-"*

"Chill," Power said cutting off Reign. *"Not around Sylph."*

"Come on nigga. I understand you're stressed right now but Sylph rides wit' us nigga. Cut her some slack and stop treating her like a baby." Reign proudly said.

Reign always believed in her. He actually encouraged her and tried to push her. Power was the only one who always tried to keep her away. She thought about the argument that

Loyalty Is Blind

they just had at dinner, and what Reign said.

"Power, she a grown ass woman. She came up wit us."

How come Power couldn't think like Reign? Sylph's heart skipped a beat. It hit her. She thought about what Reign said in her car.

"I just wanna say that's loyal. Power will appreciate that. I appreciate that. We need more people like you around. You could have done anything shady when Power got bagged, and you didn't, good lookin' out."

Reign always appreciated Sylph loyalty from the start. He always noticed she was special in her eyes.

"Patience leads to benefit. Sometimes people don't know what they got. They never notice the love that was there the whole time."

Sylph gasped and she sat up in her bed. Her eyes were wide because now she realized all she ever wanted to do was be claimed as part of the team. Power always pushed her away but Reign was the one that always believed in her and always supported her. He deserved her love not Power. Sylph's heart beat faster as she thought about everything Reign said in the past.

Sylph got out of her bed, she was on her way to Reign's.

Loyalty Is Blind

Chapter 21

Reign sat on his sofa feeling bad for Sylph. He really didn't understand why Power didn't simply let her chose her own way of life. Power could be so gangsta, but sometimes that Muslim shit hid his true self. Reign kicked his Louie V shoes off and lifted his feet onto the cozy foot rest. His phone started to ring, he took his phone off of the clip on his waist, and looked at the screen. It was Sylph calling so he answered.

"Wuttup Love?"

"I'm outside."

"A'ight, come in."

Sylph hung up. Reign thought she wanted to complain about Power. He would listen to her problems for a little while. Sylph walked in.

"Sup, Love? You a'ight?"

"I'm better. I was thinking about what you said."

"For real? What did I say?"

"About how patience leads to benefits and how the one you love might not notice till later."

"Oh, that. Yea, Power just don't realize that you-"

"Fuck Power. This ain't about him."

Reign gave Sylph a puzzled look. *What the fuck was she getting at?* He had no idea what she was talking about.

"Word? So what's this about?"

"This is 'bout you and me."

"Us?" Reign asked as he pointed at her then himself.

"Yea, Reign, us."

Reign paused. "What about us?"

Loyalty Is Blind

"You're the one who always supported me. Power kept tryin to push me away, but you always believe in me."

"No doubt, 'cause you part of our team. That's the way it is."

"I know, and I finally realized it. You the one I love, not Power."

Reign was shocked. He didn't know how to react at that surprise. What should he do or say? Of course he loved Sylph, but he didn't know if he loved her like that. Sylph was the perfect girl in every way. He was always secretly mad at Power for not being with her. *How could you let something so rare and amazing pass by?* A girl like Sylph comes only once in a very long while. Reign thought about what Sylph was saying. He shook his head and leaned down, sitting on the edge of his seat.

"Love, I think you had a lot to drink, you need to-"

"Reign, don't hit me wit' no bullshit. *I love you* and I finally realized it."

Reign looked into Sylph's sure eyes. She got up and walked toward him, and gracefully slid into his lap. Then she wrapped her arms around his neck, and rested her head on his shoulder.

"I can't. Power's my brotha."

"Power don't want me. What would you be doin' wrong? He had years and years to be with me. He never wanted it, but I'm glad for that now cuz all I want is you."

Reign thought about it. He hated that she was telling the truth, but he was loyal.

"I'm sorry. I do got love for you but I can't."

Sylph ignored Reign and gently kissed him on the lips.

"Please don't push me away. I need you right now baby."

Loyalty Is Blind

For her whole life Sylph waited to feel loved. She strived for it, and finally she felt she could have it. Reign's body yearned for hers. His mind wanted to get out of this confusing situation as his heart beat faster and faster. His mind and body battled over his loyalties. It took a lot of will power for him to gently push her face away.

"Love, I don't know how to handle this shit. This all so crazy to me."

"I know babe. It's crazy to me too, but you know you love me and now I know I love you. Please don't run from me, be real wit me baby. I can be the perfect woman in every single way, I promise. Just give me one chance, you wont be able to find one flaw in me. Give me a chance."

"I ain't doubting that. It's just this happenin' so fast and-"

Sylph put her lips on his and he was gracefully paralyzed by her soft kiss. Reign kissed back, he couldn't fight himself.

Loyalty Is Blind

Chapter 22

Power was alone that night, thinking of Sylph. He thought of all the tears he made her shed, about how bad he hurt her and made her feel. He decided he wanted things to work with her. He would take it slow, he wouldn't just put her in the mix of shit, but he would slowly work things out somehow. He called Sylph a few times but she didn't answer. That was the first time that ever happened, she always answered his calls.

Maybe she just really upset. I'll give her some time.

Reign woke up the next morning, lying next to Sylph. He felt so many emotions, guilt attacked him, and regret was next. He quietly got out of the bed, without waking Sylph, and got dressed. He went to his back porch overlooking acres, and lit up a fat blunt of weed. He took a pull of the tasty weed and blew the smoke into the warm breeze. He casually flicked the ash into the wind as he let the weed contact his mind. He thought about so many things.

Should he tell Power? Could he really have a relationship with Sylph? Would it work? Would things be awkward? Would he regret it? Would Sylph regret it? What now?

In the midst of his thoughts, Sylph walked out onto the back porch, wearing only one of his white t-shirts. She sat on his lap and hugged him close.

"Love, I think we needa talk bout this."

"Trust me babe, things will be fine, you'll see."

"But-"

"But nothin'. Don't worry Reign."

He couldn't even talk to her. She seemed so confident

and sure about this. He decided to wait it out. He would deal with this later.

Two months past. Reign and Sylph maintained their perplex relationship on the low. Sylph didn't speak to Power much. Power assumed it was because of the last dinner they all had together. Bills noticed a difference in everyone but he didn't care at all. The last dinner didn't change much for him. It only made him laugh at awkward moments when Sylph and Power would be around each other.

Sylph lay in her bed all alone. She was curled up in a ball as she cried to herself at everything that's been happening.

Oh God. What do I do?

The Cipher counted money at Reign's house. They had to reup soon so they met up to make sure everything was good and ready. Sylph walked in the room. Power shook his head in anger.

"Please get outta here Sylph," Power said.

Sylph grilled Power.

"What the hell you come here for anyways?" Bills asked.

Sylph rolled her eyes.

"That's my fault. She called me earlier and said she was gonna stop by around this time. I forgot to tell y'all," Reign lied.

Bills laughed as he looked back and forth between Sylph and Power. Power angrily shook his head. Bills stopped laughing when he took a good look at Sylph. A serious look came to Bills' face as he looked deep into Sylph's eyes and she stared back. She had no idea why he was grilling her and then that half smile crept on Bills' face.

"You aight Love?" Bills had that tone he had when he has a crazy idea or something.

Loyalty Is Blind

"I'm fine," she said, uncomfortable.

"Oh word? Then how come you was cryin' today?"

Sylph's eyes widened. She was shocked. What should she say?

How did he know?

Bills stared at her with that half smile. Reign looked at Bills, and then at Sylph, with a puzzled look on his face.

"What the hell goin on?" Reign asked.

Bills walked up to Sylph as he looked in her eyes.

"Man, sit yo ass down and leave that girl alone," Power said.

Bills ignored Power, then said. "So what up Love? You was cryin' today right?"

"Yea, so what?"

"Why were you cryin'?"

She gulped nervously. What's wrong with Bills? *Why is he always acting crazy?*

"I don't know."

Bills laughed through his half smile, he put his hand on Sylph's stomach.

"You pregnant?" Bills asked.

Reign's heart dropped at his stomach. He felt like his head was about to explode. Power stood straight up.

"What the fuck's goin' on?"

"Tell 'em Love. You pregnant!" Bills teased.

Sylph's mouth dropped. She took a step back. She was in shock.

"Is this true?" Reign asked.

"Hell yea it's true. I can tell. Me and Love got a different relationship than y'all bums."

Reign and Power ignored Bills, and they looked at Sylph.

Loyalty Is Blind

"You pregnant Sylph?" Power asked her.
Tears fell from Sylph's eyes and she answered.
"Yes, I'm pregnant."
Power didn't know how to feel. He became dizzy. He stumbled back but caught himself. *What should he do?* He wasn't ready to be a father.
"Why didn't you tell me?" Power asked.
She didn't know what to tell him. She was mad that he was now trying to show her attention.
"Power, I don't even wanna talk to you. Leave me alone," Sylph said, and then she walked out to her car.
Power followed her. Reign felt awkward. *Was the baby his or Power's? How long was she pregnant?* Power would assume it was his baby since he didn't know about Sylph and Reign's relationship. He had no reason to think different.
Sylph cried on her way to her car. Power ran up next to her.
"Sylph, wait, please just talk to me."
She ignored him and continued to her X7. Power stood in front of her.
"Stop fuckin' around. This aint no joke, this real shit. I need to talk to you."
She covered her face and bust out crying.
"I'm sorry 'bout all the shit we been through, but now I'm grown. I understand that you are yo own person and you gon do what you gotta do," Power explained.
"Why now? Cuz I'm pregnant" Now you want me?"
"This ain't only 'bout that. I been thinking 'bout this for a lil while now. I really think we can work this out and be together."
Sylph took a deep breath. She still wanted Power. She always would deep down, but now what about Reign? She

154

Loyalty Is Blind

was in a fucked up situation. She had no idea what to do.

"I want an abortion."

"I don't know about all that. I know we can work this out, we can have this baby. Everythin will be fine. On dogs."

"Oh God Power. I don't know."

"Trust me, shit's gonna change. We gonna be a family soon Love."

Sylph covered her face with her hands and cried. Power gently cupped his hand over her stomach. She wanted for Power to be right. She wanted her fantasy to finally come true. Power, her, and a newborn child. She would die for that all to be hers, but the baby could be Reign's.

"I don't know what to say." She replied.

***

The next day, Power went to Wasala's, he had to talk to him about Sylph being pregnant, and he needed to re-up. He always went to Wasala's when he needed any type of help. Power walked in Wasala's prayer room. He saw Wasala making Salat. Wasala finished his salat and looked at Power, He gave him a warming smile. Power dropped two duffle bags full of money, and hugged Wasala. A guard came in and grabbed the duffle bags.

"Your shipment will come tonight," Wasala said.

"Thank you father, but I come here to talk to you. I need help," Power said.

"What hardship has come to you my son?"

"Sylph's pregnant, she wants to have an abortion, but I want her to have the baby. What do I do?"

"You help bring that child to earth, and you receive your gift from Allah with the uttermost gratitude."

Loyalty Is Blind

"I know, but what if I'm not ready yet? Maybe an abortion would be better right now."

"In the Quran, surah 17:31 it says. Kill not you children for fear of poverty. We shall provide for them as well as for you. Surely killing them is a great sin."

Power thought about it, and then said.

"You're right father. This child is a gift from Allah. I gotta go tell Sylph to ride this out wit me. Thank you father,"

"Good bye my son."

***

The next day Power went to go pick up Sylph to talk about everything. He had to hurry up because hes shipment was about to come in soon. Sylph got in Power's Audi R8. Power drove toward where the drop off of his shipment was at.

"I think you should have the baby," Power said.

Sylph rolled her eyes and sighed.

"I don't think things will work hun."

Power took a left turn and pulled up to where the shipment was being dropped off at. He saw a big truck pull up.

"Trust me, I got this. We gonna raise this baby."

"After all of this shit-"

Power didn't pay much attention to her when he saw men get out of the truck, slide open the back, and take boxes out. He had to make sure the drop off was good. Sylph pushed his head because he wasn't listening.

"See! You aint even listenin, all you worried bout is yo fuckin money!"

Power didn't even notice he was ignoring her.

Loyalty Is Blind

"My bad Love."

They argued for a little while. She didn't think Power could change. She had to think long and hard about this. She looked at the men unloading boxes, then at Power and said.

"I need time to think about this Power."

Loyalty Is Blind

Chapter 23

Reign was in a fucked up situation. Him and Sylph didn't really talk about it much. So Reign decided he would go over to her house and talk to her about it. He drove up to her house, got out of his CLS and walked into her house.

"Hey Reign," Sylph said.

"Love, I don't know what goin' on. We needa talk," Reign said.

"I know, I'm sorry, this whole things just fucked up."

"So what you gonna do 'bout the baby?"

"I don't know. I think it's best I get an abortion, but Power wants me to keep it."

"I peeped that. Power think it's his. How you feel bout that?"

"I feel confused. I'ma be real Reign. I still love Power."

Reign clenched his jaw because deep down he knew this would happen. His feelings were hurt. He thought Sylph loved him.

"Now Power tellin' you he wanna be wit' you and you want him back, huh?"

Sylph took a deep breath, and then said.

"Yea, you right. I can't even lie to you. Maybe we both just made a mistake. We had mixed emotions, and it fucked us up."

Reign's heart hurt, he wouldn't show it though. He shrugged.

"Maybe, but who knows? I guess I feel you though."

How could she do that to him? Power throws her to the side and Reign helped her up. Now Power comes back

Loyalty Is Blind

around, and she throws Reign to the side. He didn't respect that at all. Power should have been with Sylph a long time ago. Now he wants her when Reign has her.

"I'm sorry Reign-"

"It's whateva. I'm off this," Reign said, trying to hide his emotion.

Reign walked out of the house. Sylph watched him close the door behind himself. On the way to his car, his phone rang, it was Power.

"Sup Power?"

"We gotta meet up, some shit happened."

"Where you at?'

"Come to Bills' spot."

"A'ight, one."

"One."

Reign walked into Bills' mansion. Power and Bills sat there waiting.

"What's the deal?" Reign asked them.

"Them East Side dudes are back around," Power said.

"So what? Tell Chino to have 730s take them down."

"They got some new nigga down wit em. They even went at Wasala and Hasad," Bills said.

"What? No one goes at Wasala. Are these niggas crazy?"

"They must be. It's some nigga Kadir from Africa, and he's a straight nut. I guess him and Hasad been goin' at it for a while," Power said.

Reign's blood started stirring in excitement.

Hasad.

Reign had the utmost respect and mutual understanding for Hasad. Anyone that could hang with Hasad had to be a problem. Reign wanted to see this *Kadir*. He had enough

Loyalty Is Blind

reason to go against him and kill him. Kadir was down with the East Side and he went at Wasala. Reign smiled, and he had a prepared look in his eye. Bills did his half smile.

"We knew you'd be happy, but we gotta go to this meetin' that Hasad's throwin', to talk 'bout this shit,"

"So when we got get this nigga Kadir?" Reign asked impatient.

"Don't worry, that's gonna come. I'm just as excited as you. We get to fight alongside Hasad. The man, the myth, the legend," Bills said.

Power and Reign sucked their teeth.

"He's that nigga, the colossal beast. I heard he killed six people wit' one bullet. I also heard when he was born, he cut his own umbilical cord, hopped out, and smacked his own mamma."

"Shut your crazy ass up. This serious shit," Power said.

"And now we right beside him. The greatest team in the world, The Cipher, teaming up wit' Hasad. Power Muhammad, Reign the Black Behemoth, and Hasad, the Arabian Titian. We gonna be like the Avengers!" Bills yelled.

Power and Reign both just looked at Bills shaking their heads.

"So, where this meetin at? And who's goin to the meetin'?

"We don't know where it's at yet, but everybody's goin' to the meetin'. Us, Chino and Smoke, Hasad, and a couple other people." Power said.

"Why we needa meet wit' all them?"

"This could fuck the whole city up. We telling everyone to stay out of it."

Loyalty Is Blind

"Let's go then. No point in waitin." Reign said.

*****

Everyone in the meeting sat around the table, waiting for The Cipher to show up. The air in the room was electrifying. This was the first time Hasad had a public appearance and actually showed his face. Everyone exchanged glances. A few people were scared. They only came because the meeting was mandatory. If you didn't come you were an enemy, and nobody wanted to be an enemy to Hasad. The Cipher still didn't show up, so Hasad decided to start without them.

"Now I'm sure you all heard about the attempted assassination of my boss," Hasad said.

No one knew Wasala by name. This was the first time *Hasad's boss* has ever been mentioned. That's why he held this meeting. Everyone nodded in agreement, they did hear about the attempt, and it made people think.

"Well they failed. I'm here to tell you, I know who it was, and I plan on killing anyone that they are in contact with. Anyone that has anything to do with Kadir or the East Side are all dead," Hasad said.

One of the men laughed. Hasad shot a stern glare at him.

"I failed to see the humor in my words."

"How could you call for a meeting and tell us not to be cool wit' somebody because they tried to get at you? Aint nobody tried to get at me. I don't got nothing against Kadir. I respect-"

Bang!

Hasad put a .45 bullet right in the brave man's head.

"Now, I understand you all might have shit fucked up because somebody came at me. I'm here to tell you not to get

Loyalty Is Blind

shit twisted for one fuckin' second."

No one would dare speak out of line to Hasad. Chino smirked as he looked at everyone's fearful eyes. Chino noticed only one man wasn't scared, that was Time, from The Point. The Cipher walked in, everyone couldn't believe that they showed up late. Bills looked at the dead guy Hasad just shot.

"Damn, niggas couldn't wait to get shit poppin' huh?"

"You're late. I don't appreciate that at the least bit," Hasad said.

"That's cuz we're The Cipher. We do what we want 'round here," Power said.

Chino shook his head. Everyone looked at The Cipher as they sat down. They waited for Hasad to do something but he smirked.

"Very well. Now back to what I was saying. I'm asking everyone to stay out of this. Chino, I ask that you tell the 730s to chill out for a while."

"I got you. It's done," Chino said.

"This meeting is only a message to anyone down with Kadir. I'm coming at him personally. He's a dead man. After he's gone, which will be very soon, I don't want anymore bullshit. I will kill everyone."

"I feel you. I aint got nun to do wit' this anyhow," Sammy Smooth said.

"Me too, I don't give a damn bout them East Side niggaz," Time Remarked.

Everyone in the room agreed. No one wanted drama with Hasad. They all walked out to their cars, The Cipher stood around Power's silver Audi R8, and Chino walked up to them.

Loyalty Is Blind

He dapped them up. "What's good wit' y'all tonight?"
"Shit, aint nothin planned. Why, what's good?" Power asked.
"I say we hit the casino up tonight," Chino suggested."
"Yea, we aint done nothing for a minute," Bills said.
"I'm down," Power agreed.
Reign was silent, Chino looked at him.
"You aight Reign." Chino asked.
"Yea, just thinking 'bout some shit."
"You comin to the casino right?" Chino asked.
"Yea, I'm comin." Reign said.
"A'ight, good shit. We need a break from all the bullshit. I'll pick y'all up in the stretch limo tonight."

Loyalty Is Blind

Chapter 24

The Cipher, Smoke, and Chino partied in the party bus on the way from the casino. It popping in the party bus, it was like a small club. The floor was illuminating exotic colors and there were even stripper poles in the back. The strippers danced their asses off trying to impress the five ballers. They all laughed and cheered as hundred dollar bills flew around, and the demons of greed over took the black girls lost, making them chase money around. Biggie Smalls *Hypnotize*, blasted as Bills poured a bottle of Ace of Spades on one of the hoes. Power looked around and noticed Reign was sitting in the front, on the lowest level of the vehicle by himself. He was sitting there smoking a blunt to himself.

"Yo Reign! Come back here and chill wit these hoes man!" Power shouted over the music.

Reign gave Power a blank look and waved him off like, *no thanks*. The groupies were taking so man pictures it was almost like a strobe light in that bitch. Everyone besides Reign was throwing around money like it wasn't anything to them. It was bright outside but the dark tints and the air tight, sound proof doors, hid the vision and sound from the outside world. They were happily blocked in this moving prism of luxury as the crumbling, less fortunate world went by the fancy party bus unseen.

Suddenly the party bus crashed violently. They never even heard the car screech. They only felt their bodies overwhelmingly jerk to one side of the vehicle as the lights all went out. It was pitch black. Champagne bottles broke, champagne glasses shattered, strippers fell on their faces and slid across a jagged floor, everyone was in pain and awkward

Loyalty Is Blind

positions bleeding and bruised. No one could see a thing, it all happened so fast and unexpected. No one had time to grasp what could have been happening before a bullet traveled through one window and out the other revealing a slither of sunlight through the tiny holes. Then bullets started coming one after another, faster and faster. Light beamed through each bullet hole, as the party bus rocked around from so much impact of the bullets colliding and tearing through it. It sounded like it was raining bullets on the bus.

"Everybody get down!" Power yelled over the gunfire.

Power didn't know if anyone could even hear him, he just dived to the ground in the dark bus, hoping to avoid any type of injury. There were screams, sounds of bodies dropping, glass exploding, twisted metal sounds this happened in a short moment that felt like it was forever. Then it stopped. It became silent. Faint breaths and slow body movements could barely be heard. The vehicle was now dimly lit from all of the sunlight beaming through the bullet holes into the smoggy party bus.

Power waited and listened for anymore noises of gunfire. He fumbled to his feet with a murderous glare in his eyes. Who could have done this shit? He thought to himself. Reign stood up, Bills slowly opened his eyes. He looked at Reign, who could be seen through the light of the bullet hole torn windows.

"Uhg. Reign, get down nigga," Bills pushed the words out of bloody lips with his weak lungs.

He didn't want Reign to stand up into another barrage of gunfire. Reign could barely see or breathe because of the thick air. He made his way to a door as he stepped over bodies. His lungs burned as he put his hand on the door

Loyalty Is Blind

handle. Bills saw him about to open the door, and yelled.

"Don't go out there!" Bills yelled.

Reign ignored him and opened the door anyway. Fresh air and bright sunlight rushed into the party bus. Reign caught his breath and saw that they were in a tunnel on the highway. The party bus crashed into the wall and swerved to the side blocking off an empty tunnel. Then he looked on the other side of the limo and could see the tire marks from a car that peeled off. That must have been where they were shooting from, before the shooters made a quick successful escape. Power sluggishly got to his feet.

He coughed twice. "Is everyone good?"

Power's voice was weak and worried. Nobody had the strength to speak. Bills felt like he had a broken rib and a fractured leg along with a bruise below his eye. Power scanned the whole limo. He spotted dead strippers sprawled out across the bloody floor. Bills was beat up bad, but alive. Reign stood outside trying to catch his breath. Smoke was unconscious with a bad head injury. A couple of the strippers were good, but some were about to die. Chino was filled with bullet holes. Power's heart dropped to his stomach.

Chino!

Power ran up to Chino's body.

"Chino! Wake up man!" Power yelled as he carefully grabbed Chino's arm.

Chino's eyes were rolled in the back of his head, blood poured out of his mouth.

"Chinnoooo!" Power screamed as loud as he could.

Chino didn't show a sign of life.

Allah, please help him.

Chino somehow managed to breathe a faint breath. His

Loyalty Is Blind

eyes rolled back down from the back of his head. He looked into Power's eyes. Chino barely had enough strength left to keep his eyes open more than a squint. He had only few breaths left.

Bills forced himself to his feet. He had a lot of pain in his ribs and it was hard to breathe. His leg also hurt as he limped towards Chino and Power. Reign made his way to them also. The Cipher surrounded Chino for his final breaths. Chino looked at each one of them and smiled. He could feel his body slowly fading to death. His feet were already out. Death crept up to his legs and made its way up to his waist. Chino used all of the energy in his body and soul to lift his right arm up in the middle of The Cipher, and then he smiled. He clenched his weak hand into a fist. The Cipher looked at their dying friend, memories brought pain in their hearts.

They all shared a vision. They remembered when they first saw Chino's great smile. Chino just cracked Juan in the head and looked at a cautious Cipher. Then he shrugged and itched the back if his head as he smiled so wide that they could see all of his teeth and his eyes squinted with his goofy laugh. Chino's face faded back into reality with the same smile, now on a bloody, dying face. The Cipher put the 3s up and all locked fingers with Chino.

730.

Death came over all of Chino's body.

"730 Cipher," Power quietly chanted.

Chapter 25

Chino's funeral was stressful. The church was full of Chino's friends, family, and nosey ass people. Every time someone died all of the sudden everyone claimed to be best friends with that person. All of the girls had stories of him and secret relationships with him now that he was gone. People that never had a conversation with him walked around with his picture on their t-shirts as they cried fake ass tears. Sadly, fake people are the majority of the world we live in. Chino's true kin couldn't even honorably mourn without being around all of these phonies.

Chino's little cousin Philly was there, and already missing his big cousin. Chino's casket was in front of the church surrounded by beautiful flowers and pictures of him throughout his life. A woman sang, *Amazing Grace* as everyone cried and prayed for Chino. The Cipher sat together, all dressed in $5,000 suits. Power bowed his head down as he prayed for his friend's forgiveness. They paid their respects, and walked out of the church.

It had been two weeks since Chino died. They assumed that Kadir had something to do with it, but had no idea how he could have known where they were, to attempt the hit. Smoke was in the hospital in a coma. Power noticed that Reign has been acting weird around him, and he didn't know why. Reign hasn't been talking much. He seemed uncomfortable or mad. Sometimes Reign would get in bad moods, but not like this.

Power was out of product, and it was time to re-up soon. He went to his stash spot and counted out all of the money that came back. He discovered a lot of money was missing.

That had never happened before. He was never short unless for some reason the shipment could only bring less in. Power tried to think back at what could have happened to his money. *Did he make a mistake? Did he count how much product came in? Could he have misplaced it?* Power was flat out confused. The only people that knew anything about where Power's dope or money would be was Reign and Bills. Power waved it off and decided he would deal with it later. Money wasn't really a problem at all, but errors were. Power thought about Sylph. He would go check on her and see if she needed anything.

***

Power pulled up at Sylph's, got out his Audi R8 and walked into her house.

"Hey Love," Power said.

"What's up? You look horrible, what's wrong with you?"

Power sighed before he took a seat and rubbed his head.

"I'm just fucked up right now. Chino is dead, I think I lost some paper, and Reign been actin' mad weird."

"What's wrong wit' Reign?"

Sylph already knew what was wrong with him. He was secretly mad that Sylph dropped him for Power.

"I don't know what's wrong wit' him. He seems mad about something."

"Oh, well who knew where your money was?"

"Only Bills and Reign."

Sylph thought about Power's money, and then shook away her next thought.

"Maybe you just lost it because of course Bills or Reign wouldn't take it."

Loyalty Is Blind

"Yea, I think I just lost some shit or something, but anyways what's been goin' on wit' you?"

Sylph paused, took a deep breath, then said.

"Oh yea, I been meanin' to tell you that I got an abortion."

"What?"

Power stood up and glared at Sylph like he wanted to kill her.

She started to cry out.

"I'm sorry. I was confused. I didn't know what to do."

He couldn't believe this was happening to him. He felt sorrow for his unborn child. His own seed was now dead. He didn't even understand his pain and emotions. Now, for the rest of his life, he would have to live with what could have been. Thousands of important questions Power had would never be answered. He never even got a chance to meet his own child. He was already a failure as a father, even before birth. Power never got a chance at fatherhood, and his child never got a chance at life. *How could Sylph do this to him?*

"How the fuck you gonna go and kill my kid like that?"

"Power, I'm sorry but I was scared."

"I don't give a fuck, you shoulda at least told me you was gonna murda' my seed!"

"Stop sayin' it like that."

"That's the truth. I can't believe you would pull some shit like that."

"Baby, please just listen to me. I'm sorry," Sylph said as she got up to hug Power.

"Nah bitch! Get the fuck away from me!" Power said, pushing her back down on the couch.

"I thought you wanted this to work. I thought we were

Loyalty Is Blind

gonna be together," Sylph cried.

"Hell no, not no more. You do you from now on. Stay the fuck away from me. I don't even wanna see you no more." Power said, as he stormed out of her house.

"Baby wait!" Sylph yelled as she chased Power outside, and then grabbed his arm.

Power pushed her off his arm and onto the ground.

"Don't touch me bitch. We through! You aint shit to me!"

Power got in his car and peeled out, leaving Sylph crying in the dirt.

***

Reign was at his mansion, smoking a blunt on the back deck, when Sylph stormed in.

"Power left me again," she cried.

Reign felt disappointed. *Why would she come to me with this shit? What happened to that I wanna be wit Power again stuff? How could she do this to me?* She started to whine about Power, and he listened. He fell in love with this woman and here she was crying over another man. His phone rang, and it was Hasad. *What could he be calling for?* Reign ignored Sylph and answered his phone.

"Hello."

"Sammy Smooth is dead. His body was cut up and sent back to the spot we had the meeting at. It was an example to whoever was with us. I'm telling you because I know you made good money off of him." Hasad said.

"Fuck, that's some shit. We gotta get this Kadir nigga."

Reign made a lot of money off of Sammy Smooth, and with him gone he would take a bad hit. He didn't know what

Loyalty Is Blind

he would do. He had to make some serious moves. He thought of doing some crazy shit. He hung up the phone and walked to his gun room, and grabbed his Saiga-12 with a grip poking out the side and extra drum clips. He strapped the gun to his back and left Sylph in his house alone without saying a word.

Power needed to talk to Wasala. Sylph had him all fucked up in the head. Wasala was the only person that could calm Power down. Right when he walked in, Wasala could tell something was wrong, just by the look on his face.

"What's wrong my son? What has stopped your happiness?"

"She killed the baby," Power said, as he dropped into a seat with pain in his voice.

"I'm sorry my son. Are you okay?"

"Not really. I got this real bad feelin' like someone's plottin' on me."

"Who are you skeptical of?"

"I have no idea father. It may be the cops or some random people. It could be anyone. I just have a bad feelin'."

Worry not Power. In the Qur'an, Surah 8:30 it says:

When the disbelievers plot against you to imprison you, or kill you, or take you out, they were plotting and Allah too was plotting, and Allah is the best of those who plot.

Power calmed down as he listened to Wasala. He always did whenever Wasala would quote the Qur'an. He thought about it and nodded.

"Thank you father. I feel what you sayin'."

"Don't mind your enemies. You have Allah with you and that is the best weapon."

Suddenly Reign walked into the room with a Saiga-12

Loyalty Is Blind

strapped to his back. Power gave Reign a puzzled look. *What did he bring that crazy shotgun for?*

Power stared at his friend.

"What you doin' here?"

"I'm meetin' Hasad," Reign said.

Power had a very bad feeling. He couldn't explain it, but he knew something was wrong with Reign. He looked deep into his eyes. Reign was hiding something from Power, he could tell. Power didn't feel right, so he sent Bills a text telling him to come to Wasala's.

***

Bills was cruising through the city in his Aston Martin as the song "Stuntin'" by Force the Freshest, played through his custom speakers.

He was getting road dome from Candy, while resting his arm on the passenger seat. He was holding a bottle of Hennesy Paradis and a blunt was hanging out his mouth. Ashes were falling on Candy as he drove with one hand, and tried to concentrate on the road. Candy slurped on his dick and Bills swerved. Candy stopped sucking to make sure he wasn't about to crash.

"I got this, now get back down there." Bills commanded as he grabbed the back of her head and pushed it down.

Candy got back to bobbing her chicken head. Bills heard his phone beep. He looked and saw he had a text from Power. Bills sucked his teeth and waved it off. He was straight chilling. He was having a Bills moment, and here Power was killing the buzz. Bills took a sip out of the bottle and drove down the street. He decided he would call Power after Candy finished.

Loyalty Is Blind

***

Hasad walked in the room and looked at Reign, then at Power and Wasala.

"What's goin on?" Power asked.

"Kadir killed Sammy Smooth," Reign said.

"This Kadir is becoming a problem," Wasala said.

Suddenly, they heard automatic gunfire in the distance. One of Wasala's guard's walkie talkie beeped, and they could hear a guard yelling.

"We're under fire! Its Kadir attacking!"

Power sent Bills another text that said, *Get here now!*

Loyalty Is Blind

Chapter 26

Bills looked at his phone as he sipped the Hennessy Paradis. He looked at his phone and seen the text message was really important. Bills accidentally coughed and spit liquor all over Candy as he stomped on the breaks. Candy almost flew out of the seat. She sat up alert and trying to figure out what was going on.

Bills pulled up his pants.

"Get out!"

"What?"

"I said get out bitch!" Bills yelled as he leaned over her, opened the passenger door, pushed her out and pealed out, then did a u-turn.

Bills rolled down the window as he drove past Candy.

"I'll call you!"

Power, Reign, Hasad, and Wasala ducked for cover. A dozen guards surrounded Wasala, making a human shield around him. There was a small war going on outside, between Kadir's men and Wasala's guards. Suddenly, half of Wasala's guards ran because they didn't want war with Kadir and his men. It wasn't long before Kadir's men over powered all of the guards outside. Bullets crashed into walls around them.

Kadir's men kicked down the door and ran in. Power pulled out a .45 with an extended clip and let off shots one after another. Reign pulled his Saiga-12 off of his back. He held down the trigger, and let the automatic shotgun buckshot off. All of the men coming in the doorway were torn apart on impact of the powerful bullets. The door flew off the hinges

Loyalty Is Blind

and damn near disintegrated. Bullets came back at Power and Reign barely missing them, but hitting one of the guards around Wasala. The guard fell to the ground, but the other guards that stood quickly closed the opening. Reign and Power ducked, they heard more men coming in from the back. Power dived into a roll and rolled into the doorway of the dining room, where he could see Kadir's men coming in.

Power lay on his stomach, pointed his gun out toward the men and let off shots at them. None of the men could see Power lying on the ground, which made them easy targets. They all dropped quickly. Windows broke and more men ran in, jumping through the windows. Gunfire and blood was everywhere. Reign, Hasad, Power and a coupe guards were holding shit down like an anchor.

"Wasala, get upstairs!" Power yelled, over the gunfire.

Wasala ran up his large, wide, spiral staircase, with guards surrounding him as parts of the marble railing exploded into dust left and right from the bullets. They wanted Wasala's head. Some of Wasala's men and Hasad hung over the balcony at the top of the stairs, and shot down at Kadir's men. Reign sprayed the Saiga-12 at anything he thought was an enemy. That Saiga-12 did serious damage, he had to be very careful that he didn't accidentally hit Power as they stood side by side, walking backward up the stairs as they shot at everything that moved.

Power changed the clip as he stood behind Reign. He cocked back his .45 and Reign got behind him as he shot and covered Reign to reload his Saiga-12. Reign slammed his drum clip in and they got to the top step side by side as dead bodies and limbs slid down the bloody marble stairs. Kadir's men were getting thick. Wasala's guards were dropping one

Loyalty Is Blind

by one. They began to think they might not make this one. Then suddenly a car crashed through the front wall, running over a group of men, and debris fell on more men. They couldn't see the car because of the dust. When the dust settled, they saw that an Aston Martin crashed through the wall in reverse. Bills hopped out holding a big ass mini 14. He used the car for cover as he chopped shit down. More men started to flood into the spot. Then one of the guards yelled.

"Wasala's hit!"

Power gasped and ran toward Wasala. He pushed past the guards, and stood over Wasala, who had blood dripping from his mouth.

"Father!" Power yelled.

"My son, I have little time left."

"No, Stay awake!"

The men were coming in faster and faster. Bills, Reign, and Hasad took on the beef while Power spoke to Wasala.

"My safe has a four digit code. What I saved is yours."

"What are you talking about?" Power asked.

"Uncle Wasala, don't leave us!" Hasad yelled, still shooting at the drama.

"My safe and the code-"

"What code? What's the code uncle?" Hasad asked, while he was still shooting.

"Father, I don't know what to do. These guys are too deep. They got way to much manpower." Power said.

"Don't be weak in the pursuit of your enemy. If you are suffering, then surely, they are suffering as you are suffering, but you have a hope from Allah that for which they hope not, and Allah is ever All-Knowing, All-Wise." Wasala said as blood trickled out of his mouth.

Wasala's voice was fading. He peacefully closed his eyes and went on his final journey.

"We gotta retreat!" Hasad yelled.

Reign lifted a mourning Power off of the ground and ran downstairs trying to avoid gunfire. He led Power to Bills' car. They all squeezed in and Bills peeled out. Wasala's destroyed mansion faded away in the rearview.

Chapter 27

The Cipher drove down the highway, and everyone was quiet. They were all thinking about what they would do with no connect. They still had a little bit of product from their last re-up and they all had some extra stashed, but that would only last so long. Power thought about Reign, and that look he gave him at Wasala's. *What was he hiding? Why would Reign randomly show up there with a Saiga-12 on his back. What was he thinking?* Hasad broke the silence.

"Power, you were the last one to speak to Wasala, what did he say?"

"He said something 'bout a four digit code."

"Four digit code? Did he tell you the code?"

"Nah. He just dropped a jewel, and then died.

"Well what we gonna do now? How we supposta get some dope?" Bills asked.

"We still got a lil' left. I'm not sure what to do. With Wasala gone we got no connect," Power said.

"I might be able to get some dope. I know what Wasala used to do, but I'm gonna need some money to do all that. I could never dream of putting up what Wasala used to put up. He had someone making the shit for him, and then he would pay 'em to send it. I don't get enough money for all that," Hasad said.

"This is some bullshit," Bills said, abruptly.

"We needa get at this nigga Kadir," Power said.

Bills looked at Reign, and he noticed he was silent.

"What's up Reign? You good?" Bills asked.

"I'm aight, shit's just crazy," Reign said with a plain

Loyalty Is Blind

tone.

"How come you even came to Wasala's?" Power asked.

"Hasad called me and told me that Kadir killed Sammy Smooth so I needed to stop by to get the details."

"How did Sammy Smooth even get caught slippin'? He was a smart dude. He wasn't never slippin'. You the only nigga he would ever meet up wit'." Power said.

Bills and Hasad looked at Reign for an answer, but he didn't say a word. He only shrugged with a look that said, *I don't know and don't care*. Power had a lot more questions for Reign, but he didn't feel this was the time to be getting into all of it. Deep down, Power didn't believe Reign would pull any tricky shit. *What would Reign be mad about to do anything to Power for? What Would Reign Gain?*

A black, tinted out Crown Victoria pulled up next to them, on this lonely highway. The passenger rolled down the window and a pitch black man pointed a .40 out the window, directly at Reign's head. If he pulled the trigger, Reign was a dead man. Reign sat in the back seat next to Hasad looking down the barrel of the gun. It all happened so fast. Power looked back from the front seat, and he saw the gun.

"Oh shit!" Power yelled.

The Crown Victoria drove up faster and pointed the gun at Bills, but he already peeped what was going on and stomped the breaks.

Bang!

The bullet barely missed Bills' head, by inches. The Aston Martin swerved to a stop.

"That's Kadir!" Hasad yelled.

The Crown Victoria screeched to a hard stop. Kadir stepped out of the car holding an RPG. They looked at Kadir

Loyalty Is Blind

in shock as he lifted the RPG to his shoulder, got on one knee, and aimed directly at the car. He pulled the trigger and the rocket flew at them. Bills stomped hard on the gas. The Aston Martin's wheels squealed as it moved up. The rocket just missed the Aston Martin and hit the ground behind them. It made a thunderous explosion, lifting the car up and flipping it on the hood. They landed upside down as glass and debris fell. A small crater was still on fire behind them.

Kadir got back into the Crown Victoria, and bounced. Reign crawled out of the twisted metal first. They all checked themselves to make sure they were fine. They were good, and one by one they crawled out of the twisted metal. Bills crawled out his mini 14. They coughed, and tried to catch their breath as Kadir's car drove off, disappearing in the distance. Power's mind raced again. Kadir had Reign at point blank range. *Why wouldn't he shoot Reign when he had a clear shot?* Power swore to himself that he would get to the bottom of it.

"That nigga Kadir aint no joke. I gotta kill his ass. This nigga really just pulled out a damn rocket launcher and shot at us. This is war nigga," Bills said between breaths as he crouched down, and tried to regain energy.

They saw headlights in the distance. Bills stood straight up, and when the car got near he jumped in front of it. He poined his mini14 at the driver.

"Get the fuck out the car!" he yelled.

A girl was driving by herself. She put her hands up in panic.

"Damn you fine girl, but get yo' ass out the whip," Bills said as he ran to the driver door, opened it and pulled the chick out. Bills looked at Reign, Power, and Hasad, who were just standing there.

"What the fuck y'all doin'? Get in the car."

They got in and Bills pealed out into a wide U-turn, he rolled down the window and yelled to the girl he just jacked.

"I'll call you!"

Chapter 28

The next day, Power drove down the street in his Audi R8, he was stressed out, drinking a bottle of Remy as the song *1, 2, 3 (Thousand Problems)* by Lost Boyz, blasted out of his custom system. So much shit happened to him, in so little time, his life drastically changed. He lost some money, Chino died, Sylph got an abortion, and now Wasala, his father figure and connect, was dead. The whole city was fucked up, and prices were a lot higher. 730s were like chickens with their heads cut off now that Chino was dead and Smoke was in a coma. Power thought about the moves he would make and what he should do. Earlier that day, Reign called him and said that he needed to talk to him and Bills. So much sketchy shit had been happened with Reign. *Could it be possible that Reign set up all of this shit?* Power thought about it, he also thought maybe he was just being paranoid.

Reign counted out his money. With Wasala gone, he would have to get on some other shit. The Cipher might have to get their product from of Hasad, but it would cost more than they used to pay. The problem was even if Reign got more dope, Sammy Smooth was still dead, and that was his best client. So Reign thought of a plan were none of that mattered. He called up Hasad.

Bills sat on his living room sofa with Lisa and his son Will. They were watching the action Japanese anime cartoon *Naruto*. They paid attention to the deep storyline. Naruto and his best friend, Sasuke, had a serious disagreement and they found no other conclusion but to battle. They stared each other down ready to fight. They had a brief conversation.

Loyalty Is Blind

Naruto told Sasuke to come back but Sasuke refused. They had an epic battle, but in the end Sasuke won. Naruto lost, showing that good guys don't always win. After the show was over, Will asked questions.

"Daddy, how come they were best friends but they still fight each other?"

"Sometimes people can't agree on everything, no matter how much you love them."

"How come Naruto didn't win? Why did the bad guy win?"

"That's reality son, good guys don't always win. Sasuke was too strong for Naruto. Even though Naruto was right, and wanted to save his friend from leaving, he still couldn't win. That's just the way it happens. It's real shit son."

Will thought about it, he was used to always seeing good guys win and happy endings. *Could it be true that the bad guy could win?* Will yawned, Bills looked at his tired son as his tiny mouth opened and his eyes slouched, then he closed his eyes. Bills picked him up and walked him to his bed, then turned on his night light and tucked him in. Bills watched little Will dream. He didn't even notice himself smiling as he thought about how fast Will was growing. He got on his knees, bowed his head on Will's bed and prayed for his son.

He prayed that God would make him a good father and always watch over his son. Bills stood up and walked out the room. He stopped at the doorway and looked at Will again. Bills did his half smile and closed the door. He walked to his bedroom and saw his beautiful girlfriend lying in the bed in her silky pajamas. He lay next to her, kissed her on the lips, and she said.

"I love you Bills."

Loyalty Is Blind

"You should love me, I'm Bills."

"Baby stop playin'. Say it back."

Bills hated getting all mushy. He hardly ever told Lisa that he loved her. It was just too hard to say and he didn't know why. He did love her and wanted to marry her, but he was too scared to ask her.

"Ugh, Lisa why you always on this shit? Can't we just chill out?"

Lisa laughed, she knew he loved her. She thought it was funny that every time she would bring up the *L* word, he would get all uncomfortable.

"Well even though you don't love me, I'll still always love you," Lisa said.

Bills felt bad even though he knew she was trying to get him to say it, he sighed, rolled his eyes, and then said.

"I love you Lisa."

Her beautiful face blossomed into a stunning smile, then she kissed Bills seductively. He kissed her lips, then went to her neck, and went down and pulled down her pajama bottoms. Her shaved pussy was in front of his face. He was going to do his move "Frost Bite". He called it that because when he bites it, he makes em shiver. He softly nibbled her clit, then around her pussy. She slowly slid off her silky pajama top and lay naked as Bills ate her out. He slowly licked around it as she shivered, moaned, and squeezed her titties.

"Mmmmm, Bills," she moaned.

He started to lick around her pussy lips, then licked up to her clit and licked it up and down. Her clit swelled up and he started to suck on it as he slid his index and middle fingers in. He licked around the pussy lips as he rubbed his thumb

Loyalty Is Blind

around her moist clit. He curved his fingers up inside her pussy and hit the ceiling of it, the part that feels like the top of the back of your mouth. He didn't know the official name of all of the pussy parts. But he knew how to make all of his woman moist and come. He pushed his fingers in as he fiddled his thumb around her clit and licked her pussy lips from the side. Then he flexed his fingers back and forth, curling it up and down faster and faster, hitting the ceiling of Lisa's pussy. She was soaking wet, and moaning like crazy. Bills had her locked down in his two fingers. He pulled his fingers out, he wanted to do his next move, He slid both hands under her ass cheeks and grabbed two big hand fulls. With his face in front of her pussy, he stuck his tongue out and played with her pussy as he shook his head left and right. Then he squeezed her ass tight and pushed his face in her pussy. He filled her pussy up with his tongue, getting his face all in there. Then he pulled his face back off her pussy, stuck his tongue in and wiggled it around, he got her nice and wet, then he stripped down. He got on top of his love and slowly slid inside of ecstasy. He started to pump in and out, they both breathed heavy in bliss. Lisa grabbed the back of his neck and pulled him in close, then flipped on her side, pulling him down, and got on top of him. She turned around so her back was to his face, she lifted up and slowly slid back down his dick. She bounced up and down as Bills watched that ass clap on his stomach. She arched her back and started to swerve her hips around. Bills looked at her big titties pointing up a she gave it to him. He put his hand on her back and pushed her down, bending her over on all fours, then he got up and started to beat it from the back.

"Oh Bills. Baby. Uhhh," she moaned as Bills tore it up.

He bit both lips as he held onto her waist. Her ass was jiggling every pump, and her titties jerked and swayed around. She looked back over her shoulder at Bills, then laid her body flat down. Bills pushed deeper and stroked harder as her body inched up the bed. She spread her legs wide and pushed her hands up against the head board as she pushed off of it to throw her ass back on Bills. She flipped onto her back and looked into his eyes, then lifted one leg straight up into a split, grabbed her ankle and held it down as her knee was pressed on her shoulder, then he humped her brains out. She was moaning louder and louder, she got past the point of caring to wake up Will.

"Baby, I'm 'bout to come!" she yelled.

Bills went harder, he was about to nut too. He could feel his dick pulsing inside of her. He kissed her on the lips as he pumped in and out of her juicy wet pussy, and they came together. He pushed his dick all the way in her and rested his head on her shoulder as he got every last drop in her. They both laid in that position and went to sleep.

***

Reign was at his house planning something when Sylph walked in.

"Hey Reign," she said.

He said nothing, he just gave her a plain nod. She could tell he was mad at her.

"I haven't seen anyone in a while, is everyone okay?" She asked.

"Nah, a buncha bullshit happened."

"Really, what happened?"

Reign explained about everything she missed real quick.

Loyalty Is Blind

"Well what you gonna do now?"

Reign told her his plan to save some money. Sylph just listened to him, when he stopped talking, she got to the real reason why she was there.

"What's good wit Power?"

Reign gritted his teeth. He looked at her with a serious look, and said.

"You on some bullshit."

"How?"

"You really gon come here and try to use me to get some info bout Power after all this shit? You think I even feel like talking to you?"

"Reign, it's not like-"

"Get the fuck outta here wit that bullshit."

Sylph looked to the ground, she understood where he was coming from.

"I'm sorry Reign. I guess I'll just give you time to cool off."

Sylph left Reign's spot, then he called up Bills.

Bills was woken up to his phone ringing. He looked at the clock, it was only 11 o'clock at night, he's been sleeping for a couple hours. He grabbed his phone off of the night stand and looked at the screen of it.

-Bootleg Tyrese calling-

That was Reign calling, he answered the phone, in a groggy voice.

"Yo,"

"Sup nigga, you sleep?"

"Nah," he fronted like he wasn't just sleep.

"Well, come to my spot. I needa talk to you and Power bout some shit."

190

"Aight, I'll be there."

Bills hung up, got out of bed, and stretched out. He quickly threw on some gray Champ sweatpants and a pull over super hood, then put on his white on white Adidas Yums, grabbed his .45, put it in the Champ pocket, picked up the keys to his Benz, kissed Lisa on her forehead, then bounced to Reign's. Bills drove down the hectic streets of Boston, not stopping for anyone that needed to cross the street in true Bostonian fashion. When he got to Reign's he pulled in the driveway, put the car in park and hopped out his car. He walked passed Power's car parked in the driveway and up to Reign's front door and knocked, knowing Reign always kept his door locked. Bills waited two seconds and banged on it.

Power and Reign was chilling in the living room when they heard Bills banging on the door.

"That's that fool Bills." Reign said getting up from the couch to answer the door.

Bills banged on the door again.

"I'm coming nigga damn!" Reign yelled.

Bills kept knocking on the door just because he knew it pissed Reign off.

Reign opened the door and Bills walked in and said.

"Damn nigga I been waitin out there all night. Why you even lockin' your doors like a scary ass nigga anyways?"

Reign ignored him and they walked into the living room where Power was already waiting. Bills jumped on a sofa and kicked his feet up on the arm rest. Reign sat down on his couch and said.

"You about to fuck my couch up. Get your damn feet off my couch."

Loyalty Is Blind

"No I'm about to fuck you up. I'm about to put my boot to your face." Bills joked back still lying on the couch.

Reign nodded his head and said. "Bills, I aint playin your games right now. I called yall here cuz I think we need to save money. I got a plan." Reign said

"What's the plan?" Power asked.

"We need a custom safe, one that needs three keys. One key for each one of us, and it can only be opened if all three of us open it." Reign explained.

"That sounds cool, but why you think of this now?" Bills asked.

"Cuz Wasala just died. I think we needa be safe and stash some paper just in case some shit happens." Reign said.

Power thought about it, it was actually a real good idea. Everyone could switch up their old stash spots and put all their shit together in a brand new spot.

"Aight, where we gonna get this safe?' Power asked.

"I got a couple niggas that can make the shit, y'all just gotta get your own keys so they can build the custom lock for it, then one of you can pick the stash house to put it in."

Power and Bills nodded in agreement. They all got their own keys. Reign had the safe built and has the custom locks built in. Power had a stash house with security cameras in and around it so that's the spot he chose to bring it. They put the money in and locked it shut. They lifted up the floor boards and hid the safe there. They put the floor boards back down and put a carpet over it making it look normal. Now there should be no way for Power to lose money again. Bills looked around the stash house. Reign looked at Bills as he traveled his eyes around the house.

"Aight, we good here. Let's bounce," Reign said.

Chapter 29

The next day, each one of them had something to do. Power had to gather up all the money that people owed him and that he had left. He had to count everything and check inventory to see exactly how much he had, and what he needed. Reign called Power, and told him that he was going to be out of town to go do something to get some money. And Bills was having a "Chill Bills Day," That's when he did nothing but chill and do pointless shit all day. Many "Bills moments" happened on "Chill Bills Days," So Bills had Sylph watch Will all day while Lisa took time alone to clean the house and have private time without the two wild boys running around her house. It was 8:00 at night, Sylph drove her x7 with 5 year old Will in the back. She was on her way to drop him off at home. She made small talk with little Will.

"You have fun today Will?" Sylph asked.

"Yea, thanks for takin me out today auntie," Will said.

"Anytime babyboy. You ready to go home?"

"Yea, but what's that car doin'?" Will asked as he pointed out the window.

Sylph looked where Will pointed at and seen an all-black Crown Victoria with tints, it was creeping from an alleyway, then it pulled behind Sylph's X7. She looked at the sketchy vehicle in the rear view mirror, then answered Will.

"I don't know Will. It's probably just the cops bein nosy, nothing to worry 'bout."

"Okay."

Will had a bad feeling. Suddenly the Crown Vic rammed into the back of Sylph's x6 with force. Sylph and Will got whiplash from the violent impact. Will gasped in shock and

Loyalty Is Blind

fear.

"What's goin' on aunty?" Will cried.

Sylph didn't know what to say. She had to attempt to get away from this car that just hit her. She pressed down on the gas and swerved around a corner. The Crown Vic followed, and rammed into the back of Sylph's x6 again. Will was in fear for his life. Someone started to shoot from the Crown Vic, and bullets traveled through the X7's windows.

"Get down on the floor Will!" Sylph yelled.

Will laid down on the floor of the x6. A bullet tore through the side mirror, another zipped by Sylph's ear. She took another sharp turn, then a bullet hit the back tire on the driver's side. She lost control of the car and whirled into a crash. The airbags exploded and Sylph's face rammed into the airbag hard. Will was screaming crying, on the top of his lungs.

"Are you okay Will?" Sylph yelled out of bloody lips.

Will was scared and in pain, but he was okay. She reached into the back seat and grabbed Will by his tiny hand, she pulled him up in the front seat with her, and opened the door then ran out of the wrecked, smoking vehicle as she held his hand.

"C'mon Will! Run, run!"

Will ran as fast as he could with his tiny little feet. The Crown Vic stopped behind them and four men got out and chased them. Sylph pulled out her .25 and pointed it back as she ran, then she started to shoot backwards, blind firing, hoping to hit one of the men at least. She emptied the small clip without hitting anything. Will looked back as he pushed his young legs past their limit, he saw the four big scary guys catching up fast, and they had big scary guns too. Will

Loyalty Is Blind

breathed heavy as tears fell down his plump little cheeks. He squeezed on Sylph's hand as the men gained on them. Suddenly, one of the men snatched Sylph by her hair, she gasped in pain as she lost grip of Will's hand.

"Let her go!" Will yelled as he punched the man in the leg.

The man laughed, and another man grabbed Will by both of his little arms and picked up Will as he kicked and screamed.

"My daddy gonna kill you jerks!"

The man holding Sylph by her hair looked into her eyes, Sylph looked back into his eyes. Then her heart dropped the moment she saw who it was.

Hasad.

"Hey Sylph, bet you didn't expect me," Hasad said.

"Fuck you!"

"Oh a feisty one. Haha, get your ass in the car bitch!"

Loyalty Is Blind

Chapter 30

Bills was cruising by himself in his brand new Aston Martin, as he smoked a fat blunt and listened to the song "Blunt Ashes" by Nas.

The blunt's ash falls down in the ash tray, Will I see my whole life fly past me? I'm askin' did I keep it gangsta or keep it classy? Did I? Anything else you wanna know, just ask me.

Bills blew a cloud of smoke out as he listened to Nas kick science, english and math. His iPhone rang, he assumed it was Sylph calling to see if it was good to bring Will home. Bills looked at the screen of his phone, it was Sylph. He answered.

"Dolla, dolla Bills yoo."

"Bills. What's good ninja?" Hasad said, in a joking tone.

Bills' stomach turned, he had no idea why Hasad would be calling him off of Sylph's phone, and he didn't like it at all.

"Hasad," Bills' voice was doused in rage.

"I'm with your son, he's a tough one. Here he is."

Hasad gave Will the phone.

"Daddy help!" Will cried, his voice was frantic.

Bills couldn't believe what was happening.

"Will! Are you okay? What happened?"

"They shot guns at us daddy! They pulled auntie's hair and-"

Hasad snatched the phone out of Will's hand, then said.

"Okay, now that you had father-son time, it's business time."

Bills took a deep breath, then said.

"What you want?"

"This is what you're gunna do. You will not hang up this phone on me, I will listen to everything you do. If I hear anything tricky, your boy is dead. You hear me?"

"I hear you."

"I'll let Sylph go right now, she'll go to the mall and wait so people can see her. Then I'll have one of my men bring your son to Sylph, safely in the mall. You can trust that no one will do anything stupid at a public mall. Then after that, you just follow my commands."

"How I know she really gon be at the mall?"

"She'll call you, that's the only time you can click over for a brief moment."

Bills thought about it, he had to do whatever Hasad said. It was the only safe way to save his son. He would click over and ask his son if he was really at the mall, Will wouldn't lie to him.

"Aight, let's do this Hasad."

Sylph hugged Will, she felt bad for the little guy, he didn't deserve all of this.

"I'll see you in a little bit, okay hun?"

Will nodded as he pouted, then said.

"Be careful auntie."

She nodded her head then looked at Hasad.

"I'll have my men watching you at the mall, you call anyone, then the kid's dead," Hasad said.

"Alright." Sylph said as she nodded her head.

She ran toward the Crown Vic that would drop her off at the mall, then got in. Sylph sat in the back seat looking out the window as these one of Hasad's men drove her to the

Loyalty Is Blind

mall, she got out of the car, closed the door and walked into the food court. Hasad spoke to Bills on the phone.

"Sylph's at the mall right now, you should be getting a call from her soon. I had your son get dropped off in a separate car."

"Aight. So what you want me to do?"

"I'll tell you after Sylph calls you. I don't want you telling her my plans, now would I?"

Bills' phone beeped, it was Sylph calling on the other line.

"Sylph's callin me now."

"You got twenty seconds to talk to her, you take any longer I'll have my men shoot shit up."

Bills clicked over, and said.

"You guys good?"

"Yea, there's just alotta guys watchin us right now. This is so fuckin crazy. What's happening right now?" Sylph said

"I don't know," Bills said confused. "put Will on."

Sylph handed Will the phone.

"Daddy?" his voice was scared

Will's voice calmed Bills' body. He took a deep breath, then said.

"Oh son, are you okay?"

"Yea, we in the mall. We aint gonna leave till it's safe daddy."

"Okay Will, I gotta go. I would die for you son. I love you, with all my heart, body, mind, an soul."

"I love you bigger than the universe."

Bills had a bittersweet smile on his face, he hung up the phone. Bills clicked back over to the line that Hasad was on, then said.

"I'm here, what you want me to do?"

"You took kinda long. I almost had to go to plan B," Hasad said.

"C'mon man. What you want me to do?"

"Come to the prudential business center. Don't try and bring shit in cuz you'll be searched at the door when you get here. So put your weapons away. I'll direct you once your in the building.

"Aight."

"Oh yea, don't forget to bring your key to the safe."

So that's what this was all over, the key to the safe. But how did Hasad even know about the safe. Bills had no idea, he drove to the prudential business center.

Chapter 31

Bills walked into the building, still on his phone. It was like security was waiting for him to get there because they searched him. He knew that Hasad picked this spot to meet up at, because it would be impossible to bring weapons in, and Hasad would simply overpower him by outnumbering him.

"Now that your in, walk up to floor fifteen, side B. I'll be waiting," Hasad said.

Bills did as commanded, he went up many flights of stairs, as he stayed on the phone the whole time. As he got closer to floor 15B he thought of Reign and Power, he hated doing missions without them. Then he wondered how Hasad planned this out and what he would do next. He always had a bad feeling about Hasad, he regretted letting him in close enough to do all of this. As Bills got up to the floor 15B, it got dark. He walked into the doorway of the floor 15B and found himself in a big dark office, with cubicles and small offices all around him. Bills cautiously walked down a long row of cubicles and offices with big glass windows around them. The whole place was completely silent, Bills' heart beat loud in his chest.

"Where you at?" Bills asked through his phone.

Hasad hung up. Bills looked at his phone, dialed a number, then locked it so he couldn't hang up or turn off the phone, unless he typed in the right code, then he put his phone in his pocket. Bills stood in the middle of the long hall, then he heard Hasad.

"Hey Bills."

Loyalty Is Blind

Bills turned around quick to look where Hasad's voice came from. He saw Hasad standing fifty feet away, at the end of the long row between cubicles.

Bills sneered, as he looked at Hasad.

This was him, the legendary Hasad. The most feared killer in the city. Bills showed no fear, he had a dead serious look on his face.

"I'm gonna need your key," Hasad said, with a smirk on his face.

Bills knew the moment that he handed Hasad the key, he was a dead man, but Bills wasn't going down like that.

"You gon hafta kill me to get that."

Hasad laughed, then said.

"Don't worry my friend. You'll die soon enough."

"This whole shit pointless, you need all three keys to open the safe. Why would you come after mine? By the time you try and make any moves, Reign and Power gon find out bout this shit and be on their cautious shit."

"The other keys will be no task to obtain. I already have access to one, and now I'm about to have yours. So that just leaves one key left."

Already has access to one of the keys? What he mean?

"So you set up Wasala. Why would you kill yo' own uncle?"

"That trash wasn't my uncle. All he cared about was dumb ass Power! How could he look at Power like a son, and not me?"

"So you doin all this for money?" Bills asked.

"What else would it be over? I would have let all of you live, but I never could get Wasala's safe. That old cooc wouldn't even tell me where his safe was."

Loyalty Is Blind

"So you killed Wasala jus so you could come at us?"

"Correct, if Wasala was alive, him and his guards would have caught onto my plans and stopped me. But I paid half of them off, that's how it was easy to kill off the other half."

"This is all cuz you couldn't find a stupid safe?"

"I could find the safe, I know it was under ground, somewhere around Wasala's mansion, in some spot that he thinks is important but it would be meaningless to find it without the code. I was informed if you type in the wrong code once, the safe would blow up"

"Well, fuck all that shit. I aint givin up shit. You gon hafta come get this key if you want it."

Then Bills heard a voice behind him that said.

"We thought you'd say that."

Bills quickly pivoted around, and he saw Kadir on the other end of the hall between offices and cubicles. Bills clenched his jaw. This was a real fucked up situation. Kadir was fifty feet away on one end and Hasad was fifty feet away on the other end. Bills glared at Kadir.

"So y'all was down wit each other the whole time huh?"

Hasad and Kadir was silent, then Hasad laughed. Bills turned around to look at Hasad, but he was gone, he stared at an empty hall where Hasad was standing just moments before. He looked back at Kadir, but he was gone too.

Fuck!

He braced himself as his adrenaline rushed. The silence was deafening. He would react if a fly flapped one wing. Suddenly, Bills heard a loud crash of glass coming from his upper left. Bills ducked just in time to evade a flying chair, being thrown through an office window, then Kadir rushed at him from the opposite direction crouched down in a tackling position, Bills moved to the side, dodging Kadir's tackle, but Hasad came flying at Bills with a knee to his chest. Bills quickly put both arms up and blocked Hasad but he still stumbled backwards into a tumble but quickly got to his feet. Kadir and Hasad rushed right at Bills, Bills rushed right back at them. Hasad swung a hook at Bills, but Bills ducked, pushed past Hasad and hit Kadir with a quick strong body shot. Kadir stumbled back, Hasad gave Bills a hard rib shot from behind. He almost lost his wind but he absorbed the pain and returned a strong hook to Hasad's face. Kadir hit Bills in the back of his head, making him stumble into Hasad. Hasad wrapped both of his arms around Bills arm and pulled him in, to pick him up and slam him. Bills pulled his head way back and slammed it down hard, head butting Hasad's nose, which spewed out blood, he stumbled back holding his nose. Kadir tackled Bills from behind, they both stumbled to the floor but Bills managed to get on top of him. Hasad quickly wiped off his face, he had to get Bills from on top of Kadir. Bills raised his fist up, ready to drive it down into Kadir's face. Hasad dashed at them, Bills quickly moved off of Kadir and swung at Hasad's face. Hasad's reflexes quickly made him move to the side, dodging Bills. He felt Bills just nipped him under the eye. Hasad took a step back, his face started to sting where Bills nipped him, then his face started to bleed, blood dripped down his cheek. He looked at Bills and seen that he had a big ass black Rambo knife in his hand. Hasad's eyes widened, Bills could have killed him if he didn't move fast enough. He didn't even see Bills pull out the knife. How did he even get that in past security? Bills looked at the scar he just put on Hasad's face and half smiled, then winked at him. Kadir got off the floor. Hasad gritted his teeth. He didn't expect Bills to have a weapon, Bills was definitely a slick one, he wasted no time to pull out a Mack10 and point it at Bills. Bills eyes widened, he quickly dashed to the side behind a cubicle. Hasad held down the trigger as the automatic shots tore through cubicles, windows, computers, desks, filling cabinets, and everything else. Pieces of paper scattered and flew around the room as Bills ran from the gunfire, hiding behind anything without bullet holes. Bills felt a sharp pain in his left shoulder. He looked and noticed he was shot and bleeding pretty bad, the bullet burned, and it hurt every time he tried to move his left arm. Bills gritted his teeth in pain as he hid under a desk. Hasad stopped so he could change clips, he only had one clip left, he didn't expect Bills to be this much of a problem.

"Go find him," Hasad said to Kadir as he reloaded.

Kadir walked out into the dark cubicles. Bills could hear him coming near. When Kadir walked by Bills jumped out and went to jab his knife into Kadir's side, but Kadir moved out of the way and Bills dropped the knife. Kadir's heart skipped a beat when he saw the big black Rambo knife tumble across the floor. Kadir dashed at the knife and bent over to pick it up. He wrapped his fingers around the handle, then he felt an agonizing pain in his back, he coughed and blood shot out of his mouth. He looked back and seen Bills holding a different Rambo knife, deep in his back, this one was white. Bills half smiled and winked. Kadir felt like an idiot, Bills meant to drop the knife so that he would go for it. Then when Bills saw that he wasn't paying attention, he pulled out another knife and stabbed Kadir in the back. Kadir went to fall over, but Bills wrapped his left arm around his neck, holding Kadir up in a chokehold as he still held the

Loyalty Is Blind

knife in Kadir's back. Bills left arm was still in pain from the gunshot, but he held Kadir tight. Hasad looked at Bills holding Kadir like a human shield, then he rose an eye, aimed the gun and shot at both of them. The Mack 10 bullets hit Kadir all over, Bills used Kadir for cover, but bullets hit his left arm up bad because he had his arm around Kadir's neck. Kadir fell over dead, and Bills dashed into the shadows behind a cubicle, but a bullet just hit his stomach before he could move. Hasad was out of bullets. Bills' whole left arm was done, he was dizzy and bleeding heavy out of his stomach. Hasad dropped the Mack 10 and walked toward Bills, who could barely move. When Hasad got near, Bills stood up and sluggishly swung the knife at him, Hasad easily side stepped and kicked Bills hard in his chest. Bills tumbled back into a window, dropping his knife. Bills sat with his back on the window as he bled out, breathing heavily, it was hard for him to stay awake. He could see Hasad walking toward him, but everything was blurry in his sight. Hasad crouched down and searched Bills' pockets, he found his iPhone and looked at it. He saw that Bills was connected in a phone call this whole time. Hasad tried to turn off the phone, but it was locked, so he whipped it at the wall breaking it, and continued to search Bills. Then he found the key, he smirked and put the key in his pocket. He stood up and lifted Bills to his feet, Bills was too weak to do anything but talk shit.

"Yousa bitch nigga," Bills said out of a bloody mouth. Hasad laughed then said.

"I give it to you, you put up a fight and you even managed to scar my face, but this is where you lose."

Bills smirked then said.

Loyalty Is Blind

"I always win."

Hasad rolled his eyes then said.

"Whatever. How do you win when you about to die?"

"Trust me. I got this."

Hasad shook his head and lifted Bills up over his head, and threw him straight through the glass window. As the glass shattered, Bills and Hasad's eyes met for a split second, Bills had that half smile on his face, and he winked. Bills' wrecked body fell down as the building rushed by him. He though back on his life, he felt like a failure.

I can't believe I let this shit happen. How did I get caught slippin' like that? I lived and died as a failure, I went out like a clown. I couldn't even take on Hasad.

He could see Hasad in his mind.

I never married the woman I'm in love with.

He thought about Lisa and her smile every time she would see Bills walk in the house.

I could never compare wit' my niggas. Power was always smarter, and Reign was always tougher.

He thought of Reign and Power and how they would chill on the stoop all day.

Worst of all, I never got to see my son grow up. I never got to show him the things I wanted to. I owe him so much, but I'll never get the chance to give him anything.

Will flashed in his mind, how they used to wrestle, how he used to tuck him in his bed.

Damn. I'm a failure, a piece of shit. I accomplished nothin'.

The ground came closer to Bills.

Well this is it. I hope I have a peaceful journey. God please bless my friends and family.

Loyalty Is Blind

Chapter 32

Sylph held Will's hand as they walked out of the mall. She waved to a cab, the cab stopped in front of them, they got in. She had to drop Will off at home, and go see Power. She told the cab driver Will's address. When they got to Lisa's, Sylph carried Will out of the cab and up to the front door. She banged on the front door until Lisa answered. Lisa looked at Sylph and could tell something wasn't right, She rose an eye and said.

"Yo okay Sylph?"

"No, something happened, take Will."

Sylph quickly passed Will to Lisa and walked off.

"What happened?' Lisa yelled.

Sylph ignored her, got in the cab and was on her way to Power's.

***

Power sat at his office table, wearing his reading glasses, reading through some paper work that he needed to sign for some businesses he was trying to open up. His office smelled of Muslim oils. he leaned back in his comfy chair. Something caught his eye on one of his security monitors. He looked and seen Sylph banging on the front door. Power sighed as he exhaled the blunt smoke. Then thought about what could be wrong with Sylph now. Why wouldn't she just hop off his dick an understand that he wasn't taking her back. He picked up the iPad, held his thumb on the scanner unlocked it, and pressed the button to unlock the front door. He really thought about smacking her on sight just to get his point across. She

Loyalty Is Blind

stumbled into Power's office, her face looked like she's been crying for hours. Power stood up an said.

"Hold up, I aint got time for-"

"It's Bills!" She screamed out.

Power could tell that something was terribly wrong.

"What happened to Bills?" He asked worried.

Sylph explained what she could as she cried.

"It was Hasad. He set up Wasla and is coming after you guys next. I'm pretty sure Bills was on his way to meet Hasad. It was like a trap."

"Why wouldn't you call me earlier, or drive somewhere public where they couldn't chase you?!" Power said, mad.

"I was scared. I don't know what to do in these situations. Maybe if you would have taught me some things, instead of trying to hide shit from me I woulda done the right thing! I tried-"

Slap!

Power cocked back and smacked Sylph onto the ground.

"You stupid bitch! I don't wanna hear none of that bullshit! You got my nigga in the middle of some shit!" Power was furious and knew Bills could be dead.

"I'm sorry!" she cried holding her cheek

"Where's Will at now?"

"I dropped him off at Lisa's."

Power's heart dropped, his blood started to boil.

"You did what?"

Power's voice was full of fury. Sylph laid on the floor in fear, she moved backwards.

"What did I do wrong?"

Power ignored her, he squeezed his eyes shut and clenched his hands over his head, he felt like his brain was

Loyalty Is Blind

about to explode, he was a little dizzy. The next stop Hasad would make would be Lisa's house. If Sylph was chased and let go, they only kept her alive to follower her to Will's house, because he was a witness and a major risk to Hasad alive. Hasad couldn't let them live. Power paced to his desk and grabbed the iPad. He pointed it to a bookshelf and pressed a button. The bookshelf slid to the side, revealing a large closet with many guns hanging on racks. He went straight to an M16 with semi-automatic, 3 round burst, and fully automatic options. It had an extended clip, holographic sight, suppressor, shotgun attachment under the barrel, and a grenade launcher attached mounted on the side. He loaded the M16, grabbed some shotgun shells and loaded them into the shotgun attachment, then grabbed a grenade and dropped it into the top of the grenade launcher attachment, then pulled down the latch, locking the grenade in until he needed to shoot the exploding projectile. Power held up the fully loaded monstrous gun, then grabbed extra clips, shot gun shells, and grenades, then walked toward the door.

"What are you doing?"

"Bills is dead. Aint no way he gonna walk into a trap that Hasad sat up and survive. All I can hope is that I can save Bills' family."

"Please be careful."

Power ignored her and walked out. He had no time to mourn for Bills. He got into his Mustang GT500, started the engine and pealed out. Power sped all the way towards Lisa's, with his M16 riding shotgun. He thought about everything on the way there. Now things made a little more sense, it was Hasad doing all of this shit, but how did Hasad get all of the information? From what Sylph told him, Hasad

Loyalty Is Blind

wanted the keys, the three key safe was all Reign's idea. Power found it ironic how Reign would go out of town "for money" and this would happen. That's why Power left his key at his spot, in the safe in the wall. He hit high speeds and tore down the roads.

Lisa still had no idea what was going on. Will was crying and hugging her tight as she carried him around and rubbed his back, calming him down, then she asked him.

"What's happened baby? What's wrong?"

Will explained the story as best as he could, Lisa barely understood what he was trying to say. She called Bills over and over, but he didn't answer. She began to worry.

Power parked five streets down from Lisa's house, then walked to her road holding the M16. He saw four Crown Victoria's parked near her house. He hid behind a car and watched four men get out one of the Crown Vics and start talking about something.

Lisa walked around her kitchen, holding Will as she stressed over where Bills could be, then her phone rang. She looked and seen it was Power calling, she felt a little better, she took a deep breath and answered.

"Power, what's going on?" her voice was worried, confused, and scared.

"I'll explain later, but listen up. This important."

She took another deep breath.

"I'm listenin."

"There some niggas outside yo' crib. They 'bout to run up in there."

Lisa stopped dead in her tracks and gasped.

"What?"

"Calm down, listen and you should be good. Please trust

Loyalty Is Blind

me. First, I need you to open all of the curtains in the house, and next, you need to find any gun that Bills has over there."

"Bills never brang anything in or out this house. There's nothing here," Lisa said, trying to stay calm."

"Aight, don't worry Lisa, just be calm. I can't come in there right now cuz they would see me and jus start shootin shit up, and I don't want that to happen. So open all the shades and go back to the kitchen, and try to protect yo self. Now, hurry."

"Okay."

"Insha Allah, you'll be safe."

Lisa hung up, looked at Will, then said.

"Will, mommy needs your help, go open every shade in the house."

"Okay mommy."

Will ran to the first window and ripped down the shade. One by one, Will and Lisa ripped down all of the shades, then they ran into the kitchen.

Power laid prone on his stomach, on the rooftop of the house directly across the street from Lisa's. He was looking own the holographic sight of the M16. He flipped it off of safety and put it on semi-automatic mode and aimed. Power counted out sixteen men total. Four waited in one of the Crown Vics, four went to the back of the house, four waited at the front door, and four split up, going into different areas around the house. Power had to be very careful and quick to pull this off and take them all out. If he made one little mistake then the men would rush Lisa's house. He looked at each one of the men hiding around different areas of the house. Each of those men were backup. They hid in different spots just in case the men in the front or back needed help, or in case Lisa or Will tried to runaway, they could catch them. They weren't in a group because they were scattered. The men at the front of the building would be the first to go in Lisa's, Power could see all of them fine. The men in the Crown Vic were only there for extra back up, they didn't expect anything go wrong so they just waited. The real problem was the men in the back, because Power had no way to see them unless they went into the house, he would be able to see them through the windows. Power took a deep breath and made a plan real quick.

Chapter 33

Lisa was cooking fried chicken in the kitchen. She dropped some chicken in the grease and it popped and bubbled as it cooked. She had no idea that Hasad's men were about to rush in her home. They switched their guns off of safety and braced themselves. The man closest to the door took a step back, he was ready to kick the door down. Suddenly a bright orange dot appeared on his head, but none of the other men could see the holographic dot because it was invisible to everyone's eyes unless you looked down the holographic sight. Power looked and aimed down the sight as the dot shined on the man's head, then he pulled the trigger. There was no sound from the M16, thanks to the suppressor, only an explosion of the man's head, and the bullet left a tennis ball size hole in the front door. The three other men at the front dived on the ground and quickly tried to crawl to safety. The orange dot hovered over one of the men's back, a bullet split his spine in half. One of the men got on his walkie-talkie and yelled.

"We're under fire! Enemy at an unknown_"

A bullet tore through his neck. The men in the back of Lisa's house, heard the warning on their walkie-talkies and ran in the house from the back door. There was only one more man in the front, but four men just ran in through the back door. The man in the front yelled into his walkie-talkie.

"Backup team, infiltrate from all sides!"

Little did he know, the four men that were waiting around in separate areas as backup, were all dead. Being alone in different areas, it was easy for Power to snipe them all out

Loyalty Is Blind

one by one. The men ran in from the back and split up looking for Will and Lisa, they expected their backup from around the house and in the car to run in at any second. The men in the Crown Vic opened the doors to get out. Power aimed at the Crown Vic, he took his finger off the trigger and put it on the latch of the grenade launcher attachment, he flipped the latch and a grenade shot out and exploded the Crown Vic, killing the four men about to get out. The man laying down in the front stood up and ran down the street. Power looked into the windows of Lisa's mansion, he could see that Will and Lisa were in the kitchen, safe for the moment. There was only five men left alive, counting the man that just ran away. Power looked through the window of the master bedroom, he saw a man searching it. He flipped the M16 from semi-automatic to three-round burst, aimed at the man, and pulled the trigger. Three bullets sprayed out of the M16, two hit the target in his ribs, he fell to the ground and bled to death. Lisa could hear a man coming into the kitchen. She quietly opened a cabinet below the sink and pushed Will into it. The man aimed his gun as he came around the corner of the doorway into the kitchen. Lisa swung a cast iron pan pull of boiling grease in the man's face, splashing it all over his face and neck. The man yelped and went to wipe the burning grease off of his face. His face melted off in his hands and stretched out like gooey cheese. In panic he yelled as he pointed his 9mm out at Lisa to shoot blind. He let off a shot that zipped so close by her head, she could hear it zip right by. Will ran out of the cabinet and tackled the back of the man's leg, right behind his knee. The man slipped and fell on his back, dropping his gun. Lisa picked up the 9mm and shot the man in his melting face.

Loyalty Is Blind

Power scanned the rest of the house and saw someone else about to get into the kitchen. He was about to shoot the man but then the man ran out of sight, behind a wall. Power aimed at the wall anyways and pulled the trigger. The three bullets tore through the wall, through the man, and out through another wall. There was one man left. Power heard a car coming. He looked down the end of the road and saw a big van driving down fast. The man that ran away must have got more people.

Power grabbed a grenade and dropped it into the top of the launcher, he flipped the latch, loading it in, aimed at the van and shot the grenade out at the moving van. He missed it by inches, exploding the ground next to the van, making it tilt to a lean on two wheels, but the van fell back on four wheels and kept coming. The van must have been full of men. Power quickly climbed down off of the roof and ran toward Lisa's.

Lisa held onto the 9mm tight, as she pointed it straight at the doorway of the kitchen, waiting for anyone to come in so she could shoot. She was breathing tiny, quick breaths as she stood in front of Will, protecting him with her life. Then she could hear the man just around the corner of the doorway. In reflex she pulled the trigger, chipping off a piece of the corner. The man now knew she had a gun.

He waited out of sight around the corner. Suddenly something rushed around the corner of the kitchen quick. Lisa pulled the trigger over and over, shooting at whoever rushed in, she pulled the trigger until the gun clicked. She looked at what she just emptied the clip in, it was only a jacket. Lisa's heart dropped, she dropped the empty gun, and the man walked in plain sight and pointed his gun at her. Power pulled the trigger of the M16 once. Three silent bullets

Loyalty Is Blind

hit the man up. A bullet pierced his skull and jumped out his brain, dropping him to the ground. Power walked into the kitchen from around the corner, in front of Lisa. He quickly took out the clip and put in a fresh full clip and loaded it, grabbed a new grenade, dropping it into the launcher, and flipped the latch loading it in.

"What the fuck happened Power?" Lisa asked in a frantic voice.

"No time to talk, more niggas is 'bout to run up in here."

Lisa was breathing fast and heavy, she was about to have a panic attack.

"Calm down, we got this. Pick up this dead nigga's gun and be ready."

Lisa pushed Will back in the cabinet under the sink and picked up the 9mm with shaky hands. Power opened up a window and pointed the gun at the van as the men poured out of the vehicle. He flipped the latch of the grenade launcher, a grenade flew at the van and hit the side of it, blowing it up and killing the men left inside that didn't run out yet. Men rushed in through the backdoor. Power switched the M16 from three-round bursts to fully automatic and stepped out of the kitchen, then aimed the M16 down the long dining room, at the back of the hallway where men would be running in. The men rushed in and Power held down the trigger. The M16 bullets chopped through everything and chopped a couple people in half. The men tried to return fire, but were overwhelmed by the gunfire. A couple men took cover but more men came from behind Power.

"Watch my back!" Power yelled as he still held the trigger, shooting at the people coming from the back. Lisa stepped out of the kitchen and shot toward the front door, making sure that no one would come in from behind Power. She didn't know how to shoot a gun, but she still helped. The M16 did its job by killing anything alive in sight and by keeping the men alive hiding, but the extended clip only had so much bullets in it. Power held down the trigger until the clip was empty, he pulled the clip out and dropped it to the ground. The men hiding heard the clip drop to the floor, they knew he was out of bullets. It was hard to tell where Power was shooting from with the suppressor silencing the noise of the M16, only bullets tearing through shit showed them that he still had bullets. But when they heard the clip drop and bullets stop blowing shit up, they knew. So the men ran from out their hiding spots at the same time. Power could see the men running toward him.

BOOM!

He pulled the trigger on the shot gun attachment, aint nothing silent about that shit. The men that tried to run in, split into pieces, limbs flew different directions. Power cocked the shotgun attachment back and let off another shot.

Ch, Ch, -BOOM! Ch, Ch, -BOOM! Ch, Ch, -BOOM! Ch, Ch, -BOOM! Ch, Ch, -BOOM!

Power cocked back and shot all six shots one after another. All of the men in the back were in pieces. Lisa still held down the front door, then the 9mm she was holding clicked, it was empty. Power was empty also, he had to reload his bullets, shotgun shells, and he needed a new grenade. The men at the front door could tell that they were empty, they were about to come in through the front door before Power could reload. He grabbed a grenade and dropped it in the launcher. Men ran in the front.

"Hurry Power!" Lisa screamed.

Loyalty Is Blind

He flipped the latch, loading up the grenade. The men started to shoot at them, Power aimed at the front doorway and quickly launched the grenade.

KABOOM!

The explosion pushed Power and Lisa onto the ground. The front doorway was nothing more than debris and fire. Another van pulled up to the front of the house, men jumped out and ran around back. Power coughed, then said.

"We gotta run," He said as he got off the floor. "The police will be on the way any second.

"Will! C'mon baby, let's go!" Lisa yelled.

Will jumped out of the cabinet and ran to his mother, and helped her up.

"We got no way out!" Lisa yelled over the sound of fire.

Men were coming from the back and the front was blocked off by fire and debris.

Power loaded a shell into the shotgun attachment and cocked it back, then said.

"I'll make a way out."

He walked to the side wall and pulled the trigger, blasting a big ass hole in the wall.

"Let's go!" Power yelled.

Lisa helped Will through the big hole, then Lisa climbed through and Power followed. The men cautiously ran into the house, they had no idea where Power, Lisa, and Will were. Power loaded a grenade into the launcher, and then took three grenades, and tossed them into the house through the hole in the wall one by one, a grenade rolled next to the kitchen stove. By the time the men noticed the hole in the wall, Power launched a grenade through it, the grenade flew into the kitchen, blowing up the three other grenades. Flames burst out of the windows of Lisa's mansion, wooden beams broke, rubble fell on the men, and the house collapsed in. Power, Lisa, and Will ran away into the night.

Loyalty Is Blind

Chapter 34

Power's Mustang GT 500, sped down the streets. Lisa sat passenger and little Will sat in the back. They all finally got a moment to grasp what was happening.

"Where is Bills?" Lisa asked, hoping for the best.

Power didn't know if he should tell her, he couldn't say it in front of Will. He just looked at Lisa, and she knew what it was. Her whole body was weak, she slouched in her seat and leaned her head on the window as tears fell. Little Will could tell something was wrong.

"Uncle Power, where's daddy at?"

Power ignored him as Lisa busted out in tears. Will knew right there, he would never see his father again. At a young age, Will already knew that death was a fate that every living being shared. Bills kept it 100 with his son. Now here Will was, crying over his father's death, wondering why life had to be this way. Power drove as Bills' family cried around him. He knew what he had to do, he had to go to Bills' emergency safe house. Lisa could stay there for a while, because her house was now tore to pieces. Power turned the car into Academy Homes, they all got out the car. Lisa carried Will as she followed Power into one of the apartments.

"Who's spot is this?" Lisa asked.

"This is Bills' safe house. You and Will gonna stay here for a while, till I figure out what's goin on."

"Who else knows about this place?"

"Nobody, the only people that know is-" Power stopped speaking when he thought of the only other person alive that

Loyalty Is Blind

knew.

Reign.

Power blinked away his thoughts, then said.

"Reign."

"Is Reign okay?"

"I really don't know what goin on yet."

"Oh God Power, this is crazy, what should we do?"

"I'm tryna figure that out. Hold up, wait here," Power said as he walked into a back room.

He went in and walked up to a closet and opened it, he slid some clothes on hangers to the side and saw a safe planted in the wall. He typed in the code and opened the safe. There was some money, a 357, a cell phone, a picture, and a small box that held a ring inside. He grabbed the ring box and flipped it open. A beautiful, dazzling diamond ring sparkled, glimmered, and flashed in his eyes, folded neatly in the box was a letter. Power thought back, Bills said he wanted to marry Lisa, but he didn't know when the right time would be and he didn't know how to ask her. He closed the ring box then put it in his pocket. He looked back into the safe and slowly slid the picture out and held it up to his face. It was an old picture of The Cipher back in '96. They all sat on a stoop in Academy Homes. Bills was in the middle with both arms around Power and Reign's necks. They were all smiling, so happy. Power looked at the perfect moment trapped in time, he didn't even notice that he shed a tear. He put the picture back, wiped off the tear, and grabbed the cell phone. It was an old cell phone, a Rumper, just an old flip phone hustlers use to hit plays, and it was dead or turned off. He thought of why Bills would have a turned off cell phone in a safe. He rose an eye and turned the cell phone on. It lit

Loyalty Is Blind

up and Power read the message that popped up.

-1 New Voicemail-

He checked who the voicemail was from. It was a missed call from that same day, frim the name, Ill A$$ Nigga. Definitely Bills putting that name in for himself. Power took a deep breath, then listened to the voicemail. It was kind of hard to hear but he could listen over and over to figure out what was said. It was Bills and Hasad talking.

"Hey Bills. I'm gonna need your key."

"You gon hafta kill me to get that."

"Don't worry my friend. You'll die soon enough."

"This whole shit pointless, you need all three keys to open the safe. Why would you come after mine? By the time you try and make any moves, Reign and Power gon find out bout this shit and be on their cautious shit."

"The other keys will be no task to obtain. I already have access to one, and now I'm about to have yours. So that just leaves one key left."

"So you set up Wasala. Why would you kill yo own uncle?"

"That trash wasn't my uncle, all he cared about was dumb ass Power! How could he look at Power like a son and not me?"

"So you doin' all this for money?"

"What else would it be over? I would have let you all live, but I never could get Wasala's safe. That old cook wouldn't even tell me where his safe was."

"So you killed Wasala just so you could come at us?"

"Correct, if Wasala was alive, him and his guards would have caught onto my plans and stopped me. But I paid half of them off, that's how it was easy to kill off the other half."

Loyalty Is Blind

"This is all cuz you couldn't find a stupid safe?"

"I could find the safe, I know it was underground, somewhere around Wasala's mansion, in some spot that he thinks is important, but itt would be meaningless to find it without the code. I was informed if you type the wrong code once, the safe would blow up."

"Well fuck all that shit. I aint givin' up shit. You gonna hafta come get this key if you want it."

Then there was ruffling sounds, gunshots and the voicemail ended. Power admired Bills' cunning preparation. Bills had a cell phone in his safe as a backup recording device. He could have called Power, but then Power would have picked up and not been able to listen to the message over and over to figure anything out. He thought about things that Hasad said. What did he mean when he said he already had access to one of the keys? Reign must have already handed his over because Power knew for damn sure that he wasn't giving his up. Power gasped and stood up, he thought about what Hasad said again, he said that he only needed one key left to get. That one key was Power's key, he was the next target. Obviously Reign told Hasad where they lived, they found Bills house easy. So Hasad's men would be going to Power's spot next, but Power left Sylph at his house alone. He grabbed the 357 and the money and walked out of the room, and went up to Lisa. He handed her the 357 and the money, then said.

"I gotta go handle somee shit, this is what Bills had. Take this and leave town."

Lisa took the money and gun then asked.

"Where am I gonna go?"

"I don't know. The city might not be safe for a while. I'll

call you later to check up on you."
"But I have no way out of here."
"Call a cab later, be careful. I gotta bounce."
"Be careful Power."
"I will, you be careful too."
Power hugged Lisa and Will, then left.

***

Reign was finally near the city after a long drive. He was on a mission, he slowed down his CLS and turned into Power's driveway. The door to Power's place was wide open. Reign calmly got out of his car and walked through the front door. When he walked into Power's office, he saw that the desk was tipped over, all of Power's secret compartments were opened, and Hasad's men were everywhere, still searching. One of Hasad's men sat on a sofa as he twirled Power's key around his finger. Sylph was in a corner, crying as she watched helplessly. Reign had no gun on him, he didn't need it. Sylph looked at him with tears in her eyes. Reign looked at the man holding Power's safe key, then said.

"That's two key's you got now. To keep the trust, I'm bringin the last one."

The man smirked and got up, then said.

"We're good here. Let's go."

He left and the rest of Hasad's men followed. It was Sylph and Reign alone in the middle of the ruins of Power's office. Sylph looked into Reign's eyes, then said.

"Reign, what's goin on?"

He looked at her with a mad look in his eyes, then said.

"I should kill you."

She took a step back, she could tell Reign was about to

snap. Then he quickly snatched her by her throat.

"This all yo fault! If you woulda never fucked wit me, none a this woulda ever happened!" Reign yelled.

Sylph was scared, she tried to breathe as Reign gripped her throat. He pushed her onto the ground.

"I'll come back for yo ass when I catch you wit Power."

Reign turned around and left Power's house.

Chapter 35

Hasad stood on the edge of a heli-port, on top of a tall building, standing with a big "H" with a circle around it under his feet. The sparkling city glittered under the blurry moon, with clouds speckled around the star lit sky, the tall buildings and cars were alive at night. Hasad overlooked the whole city which he now had control of. He stood there with no weapon, awaiting Reign's appearance. That's when Reign walked in the middle of helicopter pad. Hasad smiled, walked toward Reign, and said.

"My good friend Reign."

Reign gave him a plain head nod and tossed him the key. He caught it and put it in his pocket with the other two keys, then said.

"You really are an honorable man. I respect you more then anyone in the world."

***

Power ran into his mansion. When he got into his office Sylph was still there, trying to clean up and put stuff back together as she cried. Power felt bad for her, it was hard to look at her like this.

"What happened?" Power asked her.

"Reign came here, he said he was gonna kill me, said something about they got all three keys," she said as she was still trying to clean.

Power walked up to her and hugged her, then asked.

"Why would he do this to us?"

She looked into his eyes, she needed to tell him the truth.

Loyalty Is Blind

She took a deep breath and said.

"I know why he did it."

Power took a step back.

"Why?"

"Because a couple months ago, after we had that meeting at dinner, you told me you didn't want to be wit' me, so I was all fucked up. I went to Reign's and we." she couldn't even finish the story.

"You and Reign was together?"

"Yes. For a couple months. You didn't want me and I just wanted to be loved."

"That's why you got the abortion cuz you didn't know if it was mines or not."

Sylph paused, she gulped then said.

"Yes. I'm sorry Power."

Power took a deep breath. He wasn't mad at Sylph, he felt bad for all the shit he put her through. She was all he had left.

"I'm sorry Love. This is all my fault for not being able to choose if I wanted to be wit' you or not. I love you. We gotta get up outta here and just go live a calm life."

She shed a tear of happiness. She could feel that all of the bullshit was over. Her and Power would leave this city and live a brand new perfect life together.

"I love you Power. I'm sorry for everything."

"It's okay babe, let's get outta here."

Reign and Hasad stood face to face on the helicopter pad, just feet away from each other. Then wind swiped across the area, Reign looked at the scar below Hasad's eye then said.

"I was wonderin', did Bills put up a fight?"

"He was a tricky one. I definitely underestimated him,

and that cost me Kadir's life. That was a bad hit, because now everyone on the East Side are gone, I have no control over them."

"Did he have anything on him?"

"Just those two big ass knives over there," Hasad said, pointing his thumb to the side.

Reign looked to where Hasad pointed and saw Bills' knives, one with a big black blade and one with a big white blade. Ebony and Ivory, Bills claimed that the white blade, Ivory, was made from the bones of the mythical beast Leviathan, and Ebony, was forged from a meteor that crashed into earth and split Pangaea into the continents they are now. Sometimes people wondered if Bills believed the crazy shit he said.

"Did he say anything?"

"Yea, he told me he always wins."

"What?"

"Just before he died, I was letting him say his last words, and he said 'I got this, trust me' then I threw him out the window as he was smirking and he winked at me."

Reign had a flashback. Him and Bills were at an arcade, some Asian kid was beating everybody on the arcade game "X-Men vs. Street Fighter," Reign and Bills thought they could beat him, so they did rock, paper, scissors to see who would play him. Reign's rock, beat Bills' scissors, so Reign played the asian kid. He was winning as everyone watched amazed. Reign was about to win, Bills was mad that he couldn't be the one to beat the Asian kid. Reign was winning just by an inch.

"Let me get this foo. I know I can beat him," Bills said.

Reign could let the Asian kid win and Bills would play

Loyalty Is Blind

next, but he might lose.

"You sure?" Reign asked as he still played.

Bills half smiled, and said.

"I got this, trust me," then he winked.

Reign let the Asian kid win, the crowd around them looked at the Asian kid like he was Bruce Lee, no one could fuck with him. Then Bills got on the game. The match was completely one sided. Bills tore the kid's head off. Reign snapped back into reality and looked at Hasad. Bills only said that if he had something in complete control.

"You know what Bills called you?" Reign asked him.

"Nope, what he call me?"

"The Arabian Titan. He called me the Black Behemoth."

"Oh, I get it, two monsters."

"Yea."

There was a pause, then Hasad said.

"Well, now to give you what you came for," he took off his jacket.

Reign smirked and took off his pullover champion hoodie, revealing his powerful cut up body, then said.

"Too bad Bills couldn't see the great battle of the Arabian Titan an the Black Behemoth."

Ever since Reign met Hasad, he knew he was a problem, a beast, nothing to be fucked with, that's why he always yearned to kill him. Hasad felt the same exact way about Reign. Now they finally got a chance to fight it out, one on one. No weapons, no interferences, just an honorable battle between two men who held a twisted respect for each other. Whoever would win would get to keep the three keys that was the agreement they came to. Hasad put his guard up, Reign put his guard up. They stared each other down.

Loyalty Is Blind

Chapter 36

Power pulled his Mustang GT500 into a dock, him and Sylph got up and quickly paced up the wooden beams.

"Where are we going?" Sylph asked.

"My yacht, I can't deal wit' this shit, we bout to jus sail off. I don't want you in this shit, I don't even want me in this shit so we just goin in the middle of nowhere, where there aint no bullshit."

Sylph was relieved. She waited so long for this. The got to the yacht, Power jumped in, and then helped Sylph in. He turned on the lights to the luxurious floating house. Sylph went to the bed and laid down, her body felt peaceful, finally this was all over.

Power went to the computer and checked on the security cameras he had in different areas. He knew that Hasad and Reign had all three of the keys, so they would be going to the stash house soon. Power looked at the computer monitor, and could see the stash house. Nothing was different, didn't look like anyone went there that day, everything was normal.

Then Power noticed something different. There was never a doormat there before. He zoomed in on the doormat and looked at it. It was all black with a big yellow smiley face winking with a middle finger pointing out, with yellow letters under it that said.

Come in loser.

Power leaned back in the chair and ran his hand up his forehead and through his cornrows. Everything was so confusing. *What the fuck was some funky ass doormat doing on the doorstep of the stash house?* Power looked at the smiley face winking as it stuck up the middle finger. Bills'

Loyalty Is Blind

half smile and wink popped up in his mind. It must have been Bills that put that there. *But why would he do that?* It was agreed upon The Cipher to never go to the stash house unless an emergency, and even then, everyone would meet up, then go. *Was Bills trying to pull something tricky?*

***

Reign and Hasad fought like champions. The battle was long and hard, each of them exchanged blows and reading each other's movements left and right. They tried to keep their stamina, each move and thought was major.

They both tried to gain the advantage in the fight. Reign discovered that Hasad really was all that he ever heard he was. Hasad discovered the same. They both became tired, they couldn't last forever. Reign somehow managed to get the slight upper hand.

He hit Hasad with a powerful body shot, then came back with a quick jab and hard hook to his face. Hasad fell on one knee. Reign had the perfect chance to knee Hasad's face off. Then Bills' half smile and wink flashed in his mind.

I got this, trust me.

Hasad took advantage of Reign's split second hesitation and sweep kicked Reigh off of his feet, got on top of him, grabbed him by his throat, then Hasad raised his fist up, ready to knock Reign out. Hasad smiled, and then said.

"I knew you wasn't shit. You put up a little fight. But you can't fuck wit me!" he was laughing, but still out of breath.

Reign just stared at him.

"I'm not even gonna kill you, I'm gonna let you live a loser, just know that you aint shit, and you can't beat me." Hasad said.

Hasad let go of Reign's neck and stood over him. Hasad looked down at Reign at Reign as he laid on the ground. Hasad smirked and walked off, he had to go to the stash house. Reign stood up when Hasad was gone. He was mad at himself. He thought of Bills and hesitated for a spilt second. Even at death Bills could mess around with Reign. Reign walked over to the edge of the helicopter pad and picked up Bills' two knives. He really wasn't even mad at Hasad, he knew what the deal was with Hasad, but he was mad at someone else he planned on killing. He thought about where Power and Sylph would be. The only place left was Power's yacht. That would be Reign's next stop.

Power checked the other security cameras around the stash house, nothing else was unusual, only the doormat. He couldn't figure it out. He went to the closet and grabbed a 50.cal Dessert Eagle and loaded it. Sylph looked at him and asked.

"What are you doin babe?"

"I gotta go figure some shit out, and I gotta get this nigga Reign."

"Baby I thought we was leaving all this bullshit."

"I know, I know, but some shit aint adding up. I gotta hear Reign tell me he backstabbed me himself."

She got out of the bed and ran up to Power.

"Please don't do this to me babe. Why are you doing this shit?"

"Chill Love. I needa do this, I know I said we'll leave, but I cant-"

"You always do this! You always tell me one thing, then you switch up on me!"

Power placed the Dessert Eagle on the computer table,

Loyalty Is Blind

then rubbed his temples, and said.

"I'm not gonna sit here and argue with you. I need you to support me."

Sylph started to whine, Power rolled his eyes and looked away from her. He ignored her, he was leaving, he would be back later. He went to grab the 50.cal Dessert Eagle, but it wasn't there. He looked at Sylph who was pointing the 50.cal in his face. Power showed no emotion, he squinted his eyes, he said nothing. Then Sylph said.

"Behind you."

Power turned around and saw Reign pointing a .45 at them. Power clenched his jaw, he wanted to kill Reign right there. Power stood in front of Sylph, ready to block a bullet for her, Reign said.

"Move Power, this bitch gotta go."

"Nah man, you shoulda told me you was fuckin wit Love right when the shit happened, you shouldna even fucked wit her nigga, you supposta be my brotha!"

"Nigga shut yo dumb ass up and move before you get shot!"

"You shoot me, Love shoots you."

Power was right, Sylph held a 50 caliber Dessert Eagle, whatever that hit was coming off or coming out. Aint no surviving that shit.

"Shut yo heroic ass up and move!"

"Why would you do all this Reign. We supposed to be The Cipher! Who do we love? Us! Who do we trust? Us! How could you do that shit? It cost Bills' life!"

Reign's face flinched, Power kept yelling.

"Now I got nothing! Hasad has it all, he'll kill you next!"

"Hasad aint killin nobody, he just let me live."

Loyalty Is Blind

Power rose an eye.

"What?"

"Me and Hasad came up to the agreement that we shoot the ones for the three keys. I could have won, but I let him win."

Power didn't understand what Reign was talking about.

"Why would you let him win?"

"Cuz. Bills got this."

"What the hell you talkin bout?"

"Before Bills died, he told Hasad 'I got this'."

"So what?"

"I don't know man, I just felt like Bills wanted me to let him win."

Power shook his head, then said.

"You crazy Reign, you lost it bro."

Suddenly something was happening on the computer monitor. They could see a Crown Vic Pilling up to the stash house.

Loyalty Is Blind

Chapter 37

Hasad drove up to the stash house, he walked up to the doorstep and stepped on the smiley face doormat, he didn't even notice it, he walked right over it, into the stash house. Hasad's men followed him to the spot, they lifted the floor boards and found the safe with three keyholes. Hasad smiled and put in the three keys one by one. He turned one key after the other and grabbed the latch, then pulled it. His jaw dropped at what he found. There was stacks and stacks of cash, but in front was a drawing of a smiley face winking and sticking up the middle finger, under it, it said.

I always win- The Cipher 4 life! Bomb Bills Babyyy!

Hasad's heart dropped when he saw a trip wire behind the drawing. Then he noticed the smiley face had a line coming out of its head, at the end of the line was a flame, like it was a bomb. Then the image of when he threw Bills out of the window appeared in his mind. Bills' last half smile and wink was clear as day in his mind. The whole stash house exploded.

Power's jaw dropped as he looked at the monitor showing a giant pile of rubble where the stash house used to be. He looked at Reign, who was smirking, then Reign said.

"Told you Bills got this. Now move before you get shot."

Power looked deep in Reign's eyes then said.

"You wont shoot me."

Reign smiled, then said.

"You right, but Love might."

Power was confused, he stepped from between Reign and Sylph's gun line, he backed up to a wall.

Loyalty Is Blind

"Baby what are you doin?" Sylph asked worried.

"I don get what's goin on," Power said, then he quickly slip a secret compartment out of the wall and grabbed a 357 out of it, then quickly jumped back in front of Sylph and pointed the gun at Reign. Reign looked at Power, then rolled his eyes and said.

"You pussy whipped, booty blind, tender dick bastard. Stop pointing that fuckin gun at me!"

"Baby shoot him!" Sylph cried.

Sylph couldn't shoot him, she didn't know how to shoot no gun, let alone a 50 caliber, the kickback would break her hand. But Reign didn't want to shoot while she was pointing that gun at him because if she got scared and fired, Reign was a dead man. Power didn't know what to do. Reign was his best friend, he didn't want to believe that he could turn on the Cipher. Power would believe anything that Reign would say.

"What did you do all this for?" Power asked.

"You dumb nigga, I aint did shit!"

"Ever since I was missin that money, shit been changing!"

"No, since Sylph got that abortion shit been changing!"

"That shit was around the same time."

"Exactly, now think about it. I didn't take no fuckin money, I aint broke. Your precious Love took it."

Power thought about it, he wanted to believe Reign. His mind started to come up with situations that sided with Reign. Right before Sylph got the abortion, Power took her for a ride, and on that car ride, Power checked on the spot where the dope was being dropped off. He watched the truck unload the product. Could Sylph somehow saw and went

Loyalty Is Blind

back there later? Sylph could see that Power was really listening to the shit Reign was saying. Then she said.

"Shut up Reign. Stop fuckin wit his head!"

Power blinked away his thoughts, then looked at Reign and said.

"Then what you mean you and Hasad had an agreement?"

"After Wasala died, Hasad said he can be our new connect. So I called him to re-up and he had me drive in the middle of nowhere, then while I was far away from the city, he called me talkin bout Bills was dead, he wanted to shoot the ones wit me, he had two of the keys, and he had some nigga run in yo spot. That's when I went to yo crib and seen Sylph there. Right there I knew she was down wit them cuz if not they woulda killed her. She was the one that fucked everything up."

Power didn't know what to think.

"Love. This aint true right?"

Sylph took a deep breath, then said.

"This is all your fault Power. You shitted on me and kept playin head games wit' me."

Power was shocked, he felt betrayed. How could his only love in his life turn on him? Power dropped the gun and held his head up with his hands because he felt dizzy. Slowly everything started to make sense in his mind. Sylph was behind everything, all because Power wouldn't be with her. Now here Power was being held up by Sylph with a 50.cal Dessert Eagle to his back.

Loyalty Is Blind

Loyalty Is Blind

Chapter 38

After Power held that meeting and told Sylph that she couldn't be a part of the team, she gave up. She felt used, she felt like a useless piece of shit. Power fucked her, told her all these good things, and then just dropped her. She no longer would try to be everything that he loves, she would turn into everything he hated.

She decided to betray Power. Since he wanted her out of everything, she would force her way in and steal shit herself, then just leave town. Fuck Power and his doubts. He would never change, so she came up with a plan to make Reign fall in love with her. Reign never cared if she was in the mix, or if she knew whatever was going on, so she would get info from him then use it against Power in some way.

She didn't expect to get pregnant, she thought about just getting an abortion and not tell anyone, but Bills somehow found out. That changed things a little, because Power picked her up for a ride and told her he wanted things to work and he wanted her to have hte baby. But she didn't know if the baby was Power's or Reign's, so she didn't want to have it. '

When she tried to tell him that she didn't want to have the baby, he wasn't even paying attention, he was looking at a truck dropping off his product. She looked at the truck then looked at Power and pushed his head to get his attention.

Right there she knew that Power wouldn't change. So later on she went back to where the truck dropped off at, she planned on stealing the product and leaving, but when she got there, someone caught her.

Loyalty Is Blind

It was Hasad, he told her he knew what she was doing, and that they should work together to rob Power blind. She agreed and took some of Power's dope and sold it to Hasad as a pact. She thought if she could have Power lose a lot of shit and go through troubles, she would act like she's riding things out with him and he would be with her and move out of town with her. So she got info off of Reign, about the three keys and other miscellaneous things.

Sylph told Hasad anything she would find out. That's how he knew where they would be when Chino died. Reign was acting weird in the limo, because he felt uncomfortable about his and Sylph's relationship, and he didn't know how to act around him. So that caused a tension between Power and Reign, just as Sylph planned, so she could take any suspicion off of herself and put it on Reign.

When Kadir came down from Africa, Hasad teamed up with him to take Wasala out and go after The Cipher. Hasad and Kadir took out Sammy Smooth to break down Reign and make him look even more suspect, and doing that they also made it so Reign would be broke and need to re-up off of Hasad. Reign went to Wasala's with a Saiga-12 on his back because he knew people were going after Wasala ever since Hasad said it at the meeting, and he wasn't going around someone like Wasala without protection.

The reason Kadir didn't shoot Reign when he had a clear shot was because Reign was sitting right next to Hasad, the bullet could have somehow hit Hasad and he wasn't risking that, so Kadir got out of the car and purposely shot a rocket at the back of the car and missed them. Since Wasala was dead, The Cipher had no connect and Hasad said he could get them some dope.

Loyalty Is Blind

Reign was low on money and Sammy Smooth was dead so he needed to re-up bad. Sylph was babysitting Will, so she called Hasad and told him that she had Bills' son. They made a plan to act like she was being chased, Hasad promised that Will wouldn't get hurt so she agreed. After the act, Hasad got Bills to come and bring him the key and killed him. Then Hasad called Reign when he was far away from the city and told him the whole plan.

All Hasad wanted was a one on one fight with Reign, and his key. Reign had to agree, he also wanted a fair fight with Hasad. He didn't call Power to tell him because Power wouldn't believe him. Sylph went to Power's and told him about Bills, she really didn't expect Bills to die but she really wanted to get Power to leave town with her.

Power went to go save Lisa, he slipped up and unlocked his iPad and used it right in front of her to open his secret gun closet. When Power left, Sylph called Hasad and told him that the coast was clear. Hasad had Sagar go there with some men, and Sylph showed them how to use the iPad.

When she saw Reign coming in, on the security monitor, she started to fake cry. Hasad gave a strict order to not kill Reign. Right when Reign got there he knew Sylph had something to do with it, he wanted to kill her but he knew if he did, Power would think that he back stabbed him. So Reign would wait until he got both of them together. He left and went to go fight Hasad. After the fight he went to Power's yacht.

Loyalty Is Blind

Chapter 39

Lisa sat in Academy Homes, at Bills' safe house as she watched Will sleep with dried tears in his plump little cheeks. Her eyes hurt from all of the tears she shed, she cried all of the tears she could. Then someone walked in through the front door.

Lisa could hear someone coming in, she jumped out of the bed grabbed her cell phone and called Power. No answer, so she grabbed the 357 revolver off the nightstand. The man was searching around the house, Lisa looked through the crack of the door. She couldn't see the man's face clear.

She had to protect Will, she promised herself that this man wouldn't get the chance to hurt her son, he was all she had left. She slid her phone out of her pocket and pressed the redial button to call Power again. Still no answer.

The man still searched the apartment. She called Reign's number and pressed the call button, the man started to walk toward the room they were in, Reign answered the phone, before she could speak the man got right behind the door.

Lisa dropped the phone and pulled the trigger of the 357. The loud bang of the gun woke up Will and a big bullet shot out of the revolver and tore through the door, missing the man by a foot. The man rammed into the door and pushed Lisa down on his way in. She screamed and landed on her phone, breaking it and dropped the 357.

"Damn Reign, my bad for even questioning you," Power said.

"I told you nigga! You never wanna listen!" Reign yelled.

"Both of you, shut up. Reign, drop the gun," Sylph said.

Loyalty Is Blind

Reign gritted his teeth as he aimed his gun. He had to listen or she would shoot Power. He looked at Power who gave him a look like just drop it, we got this. Reign dropped the .45 by his Jordan Olympic editions, then Sylph said.

"Now get off the boat."

Reign hated how he had to listen to her. He had no problem risking his own life, but this was Power's life on the line also. He slowly backed out of the boat and got on the dock, out of Sylph and Power's sight. All he could do was hope and wait, as he felt helpless.

Power couldn't do anything, he started to feel around his pockets, hoping he had something that could help him. He had no weapons, only some money and the box wit Bills' ring in it that he found in Bills' safe. Power came up with an idea.

"So this really it huh?" Power asked, sounding sad.

"Shut up Power, you fucked up."

"But this could still work babe. It wasn't your fault Bills died. I know you didn't plan that."

Sylph shed a tear, then said.

"I didn't mean for all of this. I only wanted you to be wit me."

"I know, I know. That's why I got this."

Power reached in his pocket and pulled out the small box, he flipped it open and she saw the beautiful wedding ring. He turned around and looked her in the eyes. She was stunned, the ring was everything she ever wanted. She imagined this moment would happen for years, she started to pour tears.

"Will you marry me Sylph?"

Her tears dropped faster.

"Oh Power."

Loyalty Is Blind

Sylph loosened her grip on the gun and lowered it. Reign's phone rang, it was Lisa calling, he answered the phone and heard a gunshot and then Lisa scream before the call was disconnected.

"Lisa's in trouble!" Reign yelled.

Power quickly closed the ring box and tried to grab the 50. Cal. Sylph quickly backed up and pulled the trigger. The sound was explosive, a huge flame blasted out of the barrel of the Dessert Eagle, followed by a 50 caliber bullet that just missed Power.

He turned around and ran out of the room as she stumbled back, he ran out of the yacht and jumped onto the dock, he ran up to Reign and they ran side by side. Sylph ran out of the yatch and aimed at them, and pulled the trigger.

The bullet hit by their feet blasting a big hole in the dock. Chunks of wood scattered at the blast. The kickback from the 50.cal almost made her do a back flip, she fell back on her ass. Reign jumped over the big hole in the dock and they ran to his CLS and got in.

Sylph's arms and hands were in pain from shooting the powerful weapon. Reign and Power sped off. She sat there alone, feeling like nothing. She didn't even understand how she felt, she failed at everything, she would never be with Power, and now he knew all of her plans.

She felt like she had no soul, words couldn't explain her feelings, only actions. She slowly stood up and walked back into the yacht. She put the Dessert Eagle on the night stand and laid on the bed. She took a few deep breaths and pulled out her cell phone. She started typing out a long text message to Power.

Lisa dropped the 357 and broke her phone. Will woke up

Loyalty Is Blind

and looked at the big man who just crashed through the door, he ran at the big man but was quickly scooped and tossed back on the bed. Lisa tried to crawl for the 357 but the man grabbed her by her ankles and dragged her back.

Lisa scratched on the carpet trying to reach and pull herself to the gun, but the man kept pulling her back. Then he quickly dashed to the gun, picked it up and pointed it at her face. That's when she got a good look at who it was. Smoke. He looked at the gun in his hand, smiled, then said.

"Y'all really are a tough bunch. Bills' son aint no joke shawty. Yaknowdat."

Lisa was silent, Will sat on the bed helpless. Smoke laughed and dropped the 357, then walked up to Lisa and reached his hand out to help her up. Lisa let out a relieved sigh, grabbed Smoke's hand, pulled herself up, and said.

"Oh God. I'm sorry, I didn't know it was you. But why are you here?"

"Yea, my bad for pushin you on the ground, but I wasn't tryna get shot. I was just protectin myself. I just got out the hospital and I heard all this shit been happenin."

"I still don't even know what's really goin on yet, but how did you know about this spot? I thought only The Cipher knew."

"I'm down wit the 730s, I got lil niggas watchin everythin round here. My little nigga Philly saw y'all walkin in."

Suddenly someone ran in through the front door. Smoke quickly pushed Lisa behind him, picked up the 357 and aimed at the doorway. He saw Power and Reign standing there, giving him a cautious gaze. Smoke was relieved, he dropped the 357 then said.

Loyalty Is Blind

"Oh it's just y'all. Can someone tell me what da fuck goin on?"

Power and Reign wasn't surprised that Smoke knew the spot but they didn't understand Lisa's crazy ass phone call. They ignored Smoke's question, then Reign said.

"You okay Lisa?"

She stepped from behind Smoke then said.

"I'm fine, I didn't know it was Smoke."

They all caught up and told each other what was going on. Smoke already knew that Chino was dead, but he was shocked when he heard Bills died.

"So now no one gots anything. How we gonna come up now?" Smoke asked.

Power thought about Wasala. He said he left a safe, and Hasad said that it was burried under somewhere that Wasala thought was important. Wasala used to pray five times everyday in the same spot.

"We could find Wasala's safe, I think I know where it's at," Power said.

"Sounds like a plan," Reign said.

Loyalty Is Blind

Chapter 40

They pulled up to the ruins of Wasala's mansion in Smoke's Escalade. Power, Reign, and Smoke got out and pulled shovels out of the trunk as Lisa and Will waited in the car as they listened to "Still Dreaming" by Nas. They walked to the spot where Wasala used to pray and started to dig around. In about fifteen minutes Smoke hit something hard with his shovel.

"I think I found it!" Smoke yelled.

Reign and Power stopped digging in the spots they were at, and ran up to Smoke to help him dig. They dug around a big wooden box and pulled it out of the ground. They saw that there was a big rusted bolt lock on it, so Power said.

"We need a key, but it's rusted anyway, we can't even-" BANG!

Reign shot the lock off with the 357, and flipped the box open. Inside they saw a big steel safe that looked like it was bomb proof. They pulled it out of the box and laid it on the ground. They looked at the small keyboard of numbers on the front of it.

"We need the code," Smoke said.

"Code shmode. I'm just gon shoot this shit," Reign said as he pointed the 357 at the safe.

"NO!" Power yelled as he pushed the gun out of the way.

"What the fuck wrong witchu nigga?" Reign yelled.

"You always tryna shoot somethin. Not everything gotta be handled by shootin shit," Power said.

"You do always try to shoot shit. Ya know dat," Smoke

said, agreeing with Power.

"I'm tryna open this shit, we don't got the code," Reign said.

"Well then we use our heads nigga, this shit is explosive and here you are tyna shoot the shit. What if the bullet ricochet off the safe and hit me in the neck?"

Reign and Power argued about shooting, explosives, safes, and the probability of a bullet ricocheting off of the safe and hitting Power exactly in the neck from the angle that Reign was holding the gun at.

"Yo!" Smoke yelled, interrupting their argument.

Power and Reign shut up, then Smoke said.

"Are we gonna open this or y'all gon' fuck off all night!?"

"This nigga's always startin' a fight wit' me," Power said.

"Whatever, fuck all that shit. What did Wasala say to you just before he died?" Reign asked.

Power thought about it.

"I think something bout enemies, Allah, suffering."

"Think, Power, think."

Power closed his eyes and though about what Wasala said. His dying voice was clear in his mind.

Don't be weak in the pursuit of your enemy, if you are suffering, they are suffering as you are suffering, but you have a hope from Allah that for which they hope not, and Allah is ever All-Knowing, All-Wise.

Power repeated Wasala's deep words to them.

"That sounds like something out the Qur'an," Reign said.

"That's it!" Power yelled.

"What?"

Loyalty Is Blind

"That quote's in the Qur'an. Surah 4:104."

"I hope." Reign said.

"Just try it nigga," Smoke said.

Power closed his eyes and prayed.

Please let this be the right code Allah.

He slowly typed in the code. 4-1-0-4. The safe didn't make a noise after he typed in the code. And then it opened up. They felt like they just hit the game winning free throw to a championship game. Inside the safe were stacks and stacks of euros, fuck the cheap ass American currency. On top of the stacks of euros was information to off shore accounts. They all knew they were set for life. They jumped around and dapped each other.

***

Sylph just finished typing out a text message that she was about to send to Power. She read it before she would send it.

Power,

I'm sorry for everything. For what it's worth, I really do love you more than anything in the world. I know there aint no way for you to take me back, but I was only trying to make things work somehow. I guess I took it to the extreme. I didn't expect all of this other shit to happen. Bills was like my brother, Hasad was really the one that fucked everything up. I don't expect you to forgive me, I just want you to know my side of the story. Good luck in life, I require you to exist. Never forget about me. Your pain is my pain.

Love.

She sent the message to Power and placed her phone on the nightstand next to the Dessert Eagle. Then she picked up the Dessert Eagle and put it to her mouth, she pulled the trigger. The walls of the yacht were decorated with flesh, blood, bits of brain, tiny shattered bits of bones and body fluids.

Chapter 41

It was a beautiful star lit night on a peaceful island. Lisa, Will. Power, Smoke, and Reign were in a big mansion on a beach. They all chilled out. A lot of bad shit happened to them but they were trying to think about the good. "It's Alright" by Gambit played through the speakers built in the ceiling. Smoke, Power, and Lisa shared a fat blunt as they watched Reign and Will playfully wrestle. Reign laughed as Will jumped on his back and tried to press him down. Reign grabbed Will and picked him up over his head then placed him on his feet, then Will said.

"Uncle Reign, was my daddy as strong as you?"

Reign looked at Will like he was crazy, and then said.

"What? Yo' daddy could beat up the Hulk and Superman at the same time!"

Will chuckled as he jumped and clapped, excited, then he said.

"Really? Are you just playing wit' me?"

"For real. I aint playing wit' you."

Will was amazed, his father was his superhero. Lisa sat back and listened to Reign gas Bills memory to her son. It was so painful for her to think about Bills, she couldn't live without him. Will was the only thing keeping her going. Lisa got up and walked outside of the mansion. Power looked at her as she left. Lisa stepped off the front porch of the mansion and stepped her bare feet on the soft white sand of the beautiful beach. A warm breeze brushed by her face then swirled around her body, mist splashed out of the sea and was picked up by the wind, the mist was nice and cool as it

Loyalty Is Blind

sparkled in the moonlight and landed on Lisa's face. This was almost a perfect moment for her, but forever she would be incomplete without Bills. She walked down the beach and sat down in the soft sand as she thought of Bills.

I miss you Bills, my one and only love.

"Thinkin' 'bout Bills?" Power said, walking from behind.

"I miss him so much," Lisa said.

"Me too. He meant everything to me. I just wish I coulda told him that. I didn't tell him I loved him enough, now he's gone. I never got to tell him how much I loved him. I'm good though, cuz I know me and my brother gonna meet again on judgment day."

Lisa thought about what Power just said. She loved Bills too. She wanted to be his wife. She knew he didn't know how to ask her and that he was uncomfortable with situations like those, but her womanly pride wouldn't let her be the one to ask because society says the man should ask for the woman's hand in marriage, like men don't have insecurities. Society fucked up a lot of real people's lives.

"I feel you. I wish I had the chance to be Bills' wife. We both knew we wanted to marry each other, but he couldn't ask me. It's like he was scared to. He knew I would have said yes. He didn't even get me a present for our anniversary."

Lisa shed a tear. Power rubbed her back, then said.

"Nah, Bills did get you something. He left this for you."

Power pulled out the small ring box he found in Bill's safe, and handed it to Lisa. She opened it up, the first thing she saw was a folded up letter in the box. She unfolded it and read it to herself.

Loyalty Is Blind

Lisa,

By now you understand I'm not very good at explaining shit. Maybe I'm better at writing my feelings. Don't think for one moment that I forgot our anniversary. It's just really hard to get you a present. I was gonna get you some perfume, but you smell better than that. I was gonna get you some chocolates but you taste better than them. I was gonna get you some flowers but your more beautiful than them. I could have gave you some money but your worth more than cash. I couldn't think of anything to get you. So I just decided to get you this. The ring isn't half as important as what's under it. Watch you'll see the most precious thing on this planet under that ring. I love you Lisa. You're more special than anything I could think of.

Dolla Dolla Bills Yaaalll!

Lisa looked at the beautiful glamorous wedding ring, then lifted the layer under it, and saw a small mirror on the bottom, it was herself looking back at her. Encrusted in the tiny mirror, it said
Will you marry me?
Lisa busted out in tears. She accepted her husband's soul in marriage.

Loyalty Is Blind

Available Now

High Caliber
By **Kenneth Chisholm**

Connected
By **Kenneth Chisholm**

Coming Soon From Nautical Publishing

Higher Caliber
By **Kenneth Chisholm**

Made in the USA
Columbia, SC
04 November 2020